Dear Reader,

When I was a little girl, growing up in West Virginia, the big city represented glitter and excitement. Which is why, after graduation from college, I took a teaching job in Chicago.

Chicago is a bustling city. A city of superlatives and extremes, always emphasizing its biggests, its bests, its firsts. But the very things that first attracted me to Chicago were the same things I began to find unsettling. The Windy City never rests; it's always fixing up and tearing down.

I hadn't realized how much I was longing for the restfulness of the country until I saw Cole Murdock's advertisement seeking a teacher for the school he'd built in Strawberry, Oregon.

Strawberry was established after a discovery of gold triggered a flood of prospectors. These days, the gold can be found in cattle and the lean, hard ranchers in their broad-brimmed hats who tend them. Men like Cole Murdock.

As Cole says, part of the appeal of land is that God isn't making any more of it. Land is real. You can walk on it, see it, feel it, build a house on it. Raise children on it.

Nothing could have prepared me for the reaction I'd have to that land...or to Cole.

Molly Fairchild

Please address questions and book requests to: Harlequin Reader Service
U.S.: 3010 Walden Ave., P.O. Box 1325, Buffalo, NY 14269
Canadian: P.O. Box 609, Fort Erie, Ont. L2A 5X3

DENIM & Diamonds

WESTERN *Lovers*

JoANN ROSS

IN A CLASS BY HIMSELF

Harlequin Books

TORONTO • NEW YORK • LONDON
AMSTERDAM • PARIS • SYDNEY • HAMBURG
STOCKHOLM • ATHENS • TOKYO • MILAN
MADRID • WARSAW • BUDAPEST • AUCKLAND

To Glenn Ardt

HARLEQUIN BOOKS
225 Duncan Mill Road, Don Mills,
Ontario, Canada M3B 3K9

ISBN 0-373-88520-2

IN A CLASS BY HIMSELF

Copyright © 1988 by JoAnn Ross

1

"YOU SIMPLY HAVE to do something!"

Cole Murdock had come to the conclusion a very long time ago that there were two kinds of women in this world: those who possess true passion and those who feign it in order to win their way with a man. As he watched Molly Fairchild furiously pacing his den, Cole decided that the fiery Ms Fairchild definitely fit into the first category.

"I'm at my wit's end where Matthew Lawson is concerned," she insisted, coming to a brief stop in front of his wide oak desk.

As bright color bloomed in her cheeks, Cole wondered if Molly knew what an attractive woman she was. Of course she did, he answered his own question. Beauty was a shrewd female's secret weapon, and if there was anything the past six months had shown him, it was that Molly Fairchild was an extremely ingenious woman. Didn't she have every man in the county making a damned fool of himself over her?

Every man but two, he corrected. Him and, it appeared, Matthew Lawson.

"What makes you think I have any say over what Matthew Lawson does?"

Molly had begun pacing again, but at his softly drawled question, she spun around. "You're head of the Cattlemen's Association," she snapped. "He's a cattleman. You have to make him listen to you."

Her hands were on her slender hips, causing the stiff material of the bulky trousers she was inexplicably wearing to pull more snugly against her body. Cole felt a vague stirring and ignored it.

"It doesn't work that way," he countered quietly. "The Cattlemen's Association isn't a dictatorship, Ms Fairchild. And even if it were, I'm not fool enough to go messing around in a man's private life."

Like you're doing. He'd left the words unsaid, but there was no mistaking his tone. His uncaring attitude caused a renewed flash of anger in her. Here she was, trying to make Cole Murdock see the importance of her idea, and all he could do was lean back in that leather chair, black hat pushed back on his head, legs crossed at his booted ankles on his desk, as if he didn't give a damn about anything that didn't directly affect his stupid Double Diamond ranch.

If Molly hadn't been so upset, she would have acknowledged that Cole Murdock must have at least had the community's interests at heart when he not only put up most of the funds to build the local high school, but also advertised in professional journals in order to attract quality teachers. Previously, students in this eastern part of Oregon had had two choices—long hours of commuting, or boarding with friends in those towns that boasted schools. Neither option being very attractive, many students simply dropped out.

"What about Randy Lawson's life?" she countered. "If you didn't care about that, why did you bring me here in the first place?"

"To teach." The glitter in his dark eyes suggested she might have gone too far. "I don't recall hiring a family counselor, Ms Fairchild." He watched her fingers curl around a bronze sculpture of a cowboy astride a bucking bronc. "If you're thinking of aiming that at me, Molly, you should know that it's an original Frederic Remington. You break it and you pay for it."

She glanced down at her hand and realized that she had, indeed, been seconds away from hurling the sculpture at his smug, Stetson-clad head. Hating him for remaining calm when she was not, Molly stared at him for a full thirty seconds. "I thought you'd be different," she said finally. "I thought perhaps you'd understand."

"Understand what?"

"That Randy deserves a chance. That he's a remarkably talented young man and that talent could take him anywhere."

"I believe that's precisely what has Matthew concerned," Cole pointed out.

Frustration made her rash. "Dammit, there's more to life than cows!"

"Not around here," Cole corrected calmly. "And certainly not to Matthew Lawson. His family's run the Circle L for over four generations. Those are pretty deep roots for you to go tearing away at without fully understanding what you're doing."

"I want Randy to see that there's another whole world out there. A world that doesn't revolve around cattle."

Cole raised a black brow. "Don't you think you're being a bit presumptuous? What if the boy happens to like cattle?"

Molly had come here filled with righteous indignation, determined that Cole Murdock would take her side, which was, without question, the morally correct side. Although he was making her feel like a young girl called into the principal's office, Molly refused to back down. She lifted her chin.

"I merely wanted the boy to realize that he had a choice."

Cole swiveled in his chair, eyeing her with reluctant admiration. She wasn't playing this game the way so many other women of his acquaintance would have. After a display of feminine pique, she should have turned on the charm, of which Cole had no doubt Molly Fairchild possessed more than her share. Instead, she was openly challenging him, as she had again and again these past months. As always, Cole found her open defiance far more intriguing than practiced feminine ploys.

"May I ask you a personal question?"

Molly's attention was directed out the window at the expanse of pasture land. When she'd first arrived in Oregon, she had brought with her images of cool green forests, alpine lakes, monumental mountain peaks and grassy meadows crisscrossed by bubbling, crystal streams. And rain. Lots of it.

What she hadn't realized was that Oregon was more than that. It was vast fields of ripe wheat blanketing rolling hills that still bore the ruts of the old Oregon Trail. It was jagged peaks thrusting into a wide blue sky, the craggy rocks home to fossils dating back more than forty million years. It was irrigated valleys rimmed by rounded, barren hills.

Upon her arrival in the small community of Strawberry, Molly had learned that the discovery of gold on Whiskey Flat in 1862 had triggered a flood of prospectors who'd managed to pan some thirty million dollars' worth of ore from local streams. These days, however, the gold could be found in cattle and the lean, hard ranchers in their broad-brimmed hats who tended them. Cole Murdock, Matthew Lawson and the others were not so different from the cattle barons of old. Realizing that she had been foolish to think she could go against such powerful interests, Molly sighed softly.

"Molly?"

She glanced back over her shoulder, realizing belatedly that he had asked her a question. "I'm sorry," she said finally. "My mind was wandering. What did you say?"

"I was curious about your unorthodox attire. That outfit is not exactly designed to coax a man into acquiescence, is it?"

Molly glanced down at the stiff jacket, camouflage pants and thick boots she was wearing. Due to her exasperation, she'd neglected to change before coming here. "I can explain this."

"I've no doubt you can."

"We had dress rehearsals for the senior play after school this afternoon. Since Randy's father insisted that he ride fence, I had to stand in for him as Cassio. We're doing *Othello*," she elaborated at his questioning look.

"I've never seen *Othello* staged in battle fatigues before."

"Kids are stubborn when it comes to the classics," she said with a faint smile. "The trick is to make it come alive for them. I decided to stage it in modern dress to underscore the timeliness of Shakespeare's plot."

"Did it work?"

Enthusiasm for her pet project overcame her annoyance. "I think so. Why don't you come and judge for yourself tomorrow night?"

Aha, Cole considered dryly. Here it was. The feminine ploy he'd been waiting for. Even though he'd been anticipating such action from the moment she'd stormed past his housekeeper to interrupt his work, he found himself rather disappointed that Molly Fairchild would stoop to such tactics. Especially when he'd already decided to help her.

"Why, Molly," he drawled, "are you asking me for a date?"

"Of course not. Whatever gave you that idea?"

"Isn't it the first step?" His lips were smiling, but his eyes were not. They reminded her of obsidian—cold, black and flinty.

"I don't understand what you're getting at. First step to what?"

"Simple. You ask me out, seduce me with your feminine wiles and pretty soon I'm telling Matthew Lawson that he should let his kid say the hell with his heritage and take off to some fancy East Coast writers' commune where he spends the rest of his days penning haiku poetry, or some other equally unsalable drivel."

Twin flags flared in her cheeks as Molly tried to decide which of Cole Murdock's outrageous statements infuriated her more. She decided to take them in order.

"In the first place, I did not ask you out," she said, ticking off the points on her slender fingers. Her nails, short and unpolished, had been buffed to a glossy sheen. "So it would be impossible for me to have intended to seduce you. As for my feminine wiles, unless you count a terrific recipe for double chocolate chip cookies, I don't think I have any. At least none that anyone has ever bothered to point out."

She tossed her head furiously. "The only reason I asked you to help me talk some sense into Matthew Lawson is that you've been to college, so you know the benefits of learning about other worlds, other lifestyles. Which brings us to Randy's writing." She reached into a folder she'd laid on his desk and pulled out a sheaf of notebook paper covered in a wide, looping scrawl. "When, and if, you ever decide to come down off your high horse, Mr. Murdock, I'd suggest you read these and see exactly how deeply Randy feels about this country."

As she waved the papers under his nose, her hands trembled with emotion. "Read how much he loves the land. Not to mention those damned cattle you all hold in such ridiculous esteem."

"Molly—"

"Ms Fairchild to you. I only allow my friends to call me Molly." With that she marched out of the room. A moment later Cole heard the front door slam.

"Congratulations. I see you haven't lost your touch with the ladies," a husky feminine voice drawled.

Cole, whose attention had been drawn out the window by the sway of Molly's camouflage-covered hips as she'd stormed toward her bright yellow Pontiac Sunbird, scowled at the interruption.

"Some ladies are pricklier than others," he said grumpily.

Dallas Cameron had been housekeeper at the Double Diamond for over forty years, long enough that she didn't feel any need to stand on ceremony. "From what I hear, that child is about as sweet as they come."

"That *child* happens to be twenty-six," Cole pointed out. "As for sweet..." He shrugged. "You'd better check and make certain she didn't break half the windows in the house."

"She did look a mite riled up," Dallas agreed. "What did she want?"

"She wanted me to read some papers written by one of her students."

The woman's eyes narrowed suspiciously as she folded her arms over her ample bosom. "I may just be the housekeeper around this spread, but don't you be forgetting that I raised you from a pup, Cole Murdock. So save your lies for some foolish woman who'll believe them."

Cole threw back his head and laughed, as he was supposed to. Dallas was much more than a housekeeper and the wife of the Double Diamond's foreman, Merle; she was the closest thing he'd ever known to a mother. His own mother had never taken to ranch life. Shortly after his first birthday, Isabel Murdock had packed her bags and left without a backward glance. If Garrett Murdock had missed his lovely blond wife, he never mentioned it. After all, Isabel had lived up to her part of the bargain when she'd presented him with a son and heir. Someone to carry on the family tradition.

"You always could see right through me."

Dallas grinned, flashing a bright gold tooth in a weathered face. "I can tell that Molly Fairchild's gotten under your skin," she countered. "The only thing I haven't been able to figure out is what took you so long to get interested. It's been six months since you brought her here to teach at the school."

"I know how long it's been," Cole returned. "Since she's been bombarding me with wild ideas nearly every day of those months on some new project she wants to initiate. And for your information, I'm not interested."

"Aren't you?"

"Hell, no," he insisted. "Besides, even if I was interested, I'd have had to fight my way through half the county. The woman's been more popular than a keg of ice-cold beer at branding time."

"You seem to be mighty observant, for a man who isn't interested."

"I don't remember saying I was blind," Cole retorted.

"You're not gettin' any younger, boy. I'd say it's about time you started looking around for a wife." Her smile was absolutely guileless. "Mebbe one like Molly."

"I've already had one wife, Dallas. I'm not in the market for another."

His firm tone brooked no further discussion. Heaving an exaggerated sigh of frustration, Dallas left him to the breeding records he'd been going over before Molly Fairchild had burst into the office.

It was going to be a good season. Goliath, the huge Simmental bull he'd purchased, would see to that. The regal dark red-and-white bull had already shown himself to be quite the Don Juan, and a new batch of leaner, rapidly growing calves had already proven his fertility.

"You keep it up and we're going to have ourselves a good year, Goliath, old boy," Cole murmured as he studied a glossy photo of the champion bull. "A very good year."

Putting the file aside, his gaze settled on the papers Molly had left behind. Telling himself that it was only mild curiosity, he began to read.

THE TELEPHONE WAS RINGING when Molly reached her house. The sense of foreboding she experienced could have come from lingering vestiges of her argument with Cole Murdock. Or, Molly considered grimly as she picked up the receiver, it could be her intuition that always seemed to recognize Loretta Belle's ring. As usual her intuition was right.

"Yes, operator," she said, trying to stifle her sigh. "I'll accept the charges."

"Molly. It's about time you answered your phone," a female voice complained. "I've been trying to reach you for hours."

"I was out." She sank wearily onto a nearby chair, preparing herself for the usual litany of complaints.

"Having fun, no doubt. While I was stuck here in this torture chamber." The grievous tone sharpened the woman's soft West Virginia drawl, so similar to Molly's own accent.

"It's not a torture chamber," Molly answered automatically. They'd been through this before.

"How could you possibly know what it's like? When you're all the way out there in Oregon, living in the lap of luxury?"

Molly glanced around the room. The white frame house that she shared with two other teachers in town was comfortable and roomy. But it certainly could never be described as luxurious. Molly, however, knew better than to argue.

"What did you call for, Loretta?"

"Is it a crime to want someone to talk to?"

"We talked this past Sunday," Molly reminded her. "Remember? I called you. Like I do every Sunday."

"Calling isn't good enough. I want you to come rescue me. Now."

Molly briefly closed her eyes, garnering strength. "Rescue you from what?"

"The plot Dr. Wickes and these nefarious nurses have cooked up against me, of course."

"Plot?"

"They're planning to torture me, Molly."

"Dr. Wickes is a very nice woman," Molly argued patiently. "And an excellent doctor. She would never torture anyone."

"She's going to. I heard them talking," Loretta Belle insisted. "They're going to give me drugs, Molly."

"That's what your doctors are supposed to do. We've discussed this before, Loretta. If you want to get better, you have to stay on your medicine."

"Not that medicine. These are mind-altering drugs. Like in that movie I saw last night on cable."

Molly had a sinking feeling deep in her stomach. It had taken a week to calm Loretta down after she had watched *The Invasion of the Body Snatchers* last December. Molly had just arrived at the sanatorium Christmas party with an armful of presents when Loretta, convinced that the younger woman was one of the "pod people," had tried to knock her out with a folding chair.

"What movie?"

"I forget its name. But Jack Nicholson was in it. Along with a sadistic nurse who looked exactly like Dr. Wickes. And they were drugging all the patients."

"*One Flew Over the Cuckoo's Nest.*" Molly suddenly had a very good idea where this latest conspiracy idea had come from. She made a mental note to ask the staff to monitor Loretta's television viewing more carefully.

"What?"

"That was the name of the movie. It wasn't real life, Loretta."

"It was damned near close enough for me. That's probably where Dr. Wickes got the idea to give me the drugs. Molly, they're going to force me to say that Johnny Cash is a Communist. And that he and the Russians are planning to take over the country!"

Molly told herself that she should have grown used to Loretta Belle's delusions by now. And for the most part she had. Still, this was, without a doubt, one of the more colorful ones she'd heard over the years. "Johnny Cash is a Communist?"

"Of course he isn't," Loretta Belle returned sharply. "But Dr. Wickes is trying to discredit him before the entire country. Don't you see? By using drugs she can get me to turn against one of my own." Her tremulous voice rose several octaves. "I swear I'll cut my wrists before I'd allow that to happen, Molly!"

Although the skin on the inside of Loretta Belle's wrists already looked like railroad tracks from previous dramatic suicide attempts, Molly lived with the very real fear that the next time she might actually succeed.

"Why don't I call Dr. Wickes and discuss this with her?"

"She'll lie. They all lie. Just like that nurse on the movie last night."

Sometimes Molly secretly suspected Loretta Belle of possessing ESP. Her knack for knowing precisely when she would most disrupt Molly's life was uncanny. Here she was, with the play tomorrow night and the issue of

Randy's college left unsettled, and she was going to have to fly back to West Virginia for what experience had taught her would be a futile visit. By the time she arrived at the sanatorium, Loretta Belle would have forgotten both this call and the perceived plot. Still, she had no choice.

"All right. I'll try to get a plane out tonight."

"Don't bother." The voice on the other end of the long-distance telephone line had turned frosty. "You're probably on her side, anyway. I want Billy Joe to come. *He* cares about what happens to me."

"I care about you."

Loretta Belle ignored Molly's soft declaration. "I want Billy Joe," she demanded. "Are you going to call him? Or shall I? That is, if they don't discover that I've sneaked out of my room to use this phone and shoot me down like a ring-tailed possum before I can dial the operator again."

"No one is going to shoot you," Molly insisted firmly. "Now why don't you go back to your room and I'll call Billy Joe."

"Do you promise?"

"Cross my heart."

There was a lengthy silence as she seemed to be thinking Molly's words over. "All right. But if Billy Joe finds me drugged and tied to my bed telling hordes of reporters that Johnny Cash is a Russian, it's on your head," she said as she hung up the telephone.

Molly shook her head in mute frustration as a dial tone replaced the grievous voice. Loretta Belle's real name was Sarah Jane Pence. She was also Molly's mother.

Loretta had had a lot of dreams while growing up in the hill country of West Virginia. Big dreams. Dreams no one around Coal City seemed to be able to appreciate.

She was going to be a famous country star. When she was a young girl, she'd spent every Saturday night singing along with radio WWVA's *Wheeling Feeling, Jamboree USA* and imagining Buddy Ray introducing her to all her screaming fans. After conquering Wheeling, she'd take Nashville by storm. Later, since she'd never heard of anyone famous with a boring old name like Sarah, she changed it to that of her favorite singer— Loretta Lynn—for luck. Sarah figured that if Loretta Lynn could make it out of coal country, so could she. She chose Belle for her new last name because she thought it was pretty and kind of musical.

Loretta Belle never did make it to Nashville. Nor did she make it to Wheeling. Actually, although she managed to get a few singing jobs, she never quite got past Clarksburg. Oh, she made lots of plans over the years, but something always seemed to get in her way. Men. Alcohol. And the fear that her lifelong dream might be no more substantial than the morning fog that hovered over the Allegheny Mountains.

This fear was so terrifying and so deeply ingrained that Loretta would only admit it to herself on those dark, lonely nights when she was forced to sleep alone. Which wasn't very often. So no one who knew Loretta was very surprised when she became pregnant during a brief stint singing and waiting tables at a bar just outside Logan.

Although Loretta had a great many dreams, becoming a mother definitely wasn't one of them. In desperation she turned to a local herbalist who, for twenty dollars, sold her a "guaranteed cure" for her dilemma. Instead of solving her problem, the noxious concoction gave Loretta Belle hallucinations that had her screaming in terror for three days as she tossed and turned on sweat-soaked sheets. Seven months later she gave birth to a baby girl whom she promptly abandoned to a nearby Catholic services organization.

Molly had been nine when Ellen Pence, a distant cousin of her mother's, had shown up at the orphanage because she needed a young girl to help with chores around the house. Twelve children and a recent hysterectomy had left Ellen weak and unable to care for her family single-handedly. Although the days were long and there was never any money for the extra little trinkets young girls like, the family did their best to make Molly feel like one of their own.

One of the Pence boys, Billy Joe, was only a few months older than Molly, and it wasn't long before the two became close friends. Later their relationship escalated to that of high-school sweethearts, but the teenage romance ebbed after Molly went off to college. One thing that had never changed, however, was that Billy Joe had remained, even after all these years, Molly's best friend.

Loretta had never shown any interest in the child she'd borne, but when her alcoholism made it impossible for her to care for herself any longer, Molly, who had always been aware of who her mother was, had immediately stepped in, arranging for Loretta's admission to a private sanatorium in Charleston. That had been five long years ago, and not a moment of it had been easy on anyone.

Although Molly faithfully visited her mother during every vacation and telephoned once a week, Loretta continued to call with a litany of imagined grievances. While Molly and the staff constantly tried to appease Loretta Belle, their efforts often proved futile. It was then that, despite her failing health, Loretta would manage to escape the hospital grounds and disappear for days, weeks, often months, at a time.

Inevitably she would end up at her childhood home, now owned by Billy Joe. Uncomplaining, Billy Joe would take her back to the hospital, and the cycle would begin again.

In the beginning Molly had immediately returned home on each of these occasions, but the delusions which were taking over more and more of Loretta's mind had convinced her that her problems were all Molly's fault. Things had deteriorated to the point that after the Christmas party fiasco, Dr. Janet Wickes had suggested that Molly seriously consider no longer coming to the sanatorium. It would make things easier, the doctor had told her kindly, for both mother and daughter.

Molly sighed deeply. A minute later she was dialing the number she knew by heart.

"Billy Joe." Molly immediately had a sense of relief at hearing the deep, familiar voice that answered the telephone. "She's going off the deep end again. This time they're trying to make her tell the world that Johnny Cash is a Communist."

She did her best to smile and failed miserably. "You know, if I wasn't so close to the situation, I just might find this latest delusion funny. I mean, Johnny Cash, of all people? That's even worse than the one about Jerry Lee Lewis asking her to record an album with him last month. How in the world does she come up with these things?" Her voice cracked and Molly could have wept as she listened to the calm, reassuring words. "What would I ever do without you?" she wondered aloud.

Again those warm, wonderful words.

"Yes, I know you'll take care of everything. You always do." A single tear slid down her cheek. "I love you, Billy Joe Pence," Molly whispered as she hung up.

2

MOLLY WAS WRITING ON THE chalkboard, her back to the door, when Cole entered her classroom late the following afternoon. The sudden murmur of excited conversation caught her attention and she turned, surprised and not a little uneasy when she found him standing only inches away.

"Mr. Murdock," she greeted him with a nod. "What a pleasant surprise."

Her voice was calm, but her green eyes were not. Cole found himself once again unwillingly intrigued by the thought of so much barely restrained passion. The woman must do daily battle with her emotions, he mused.

"I was driving by the school and realized how long it's been since I dropped in for an official visit."

Molly got the message, loud and clear. This was merely his way of reminding her who had hired her. And who could fire her. "If I'd known you were coming, I would have arranged something more to your liking than the discussion of Robert Frost scheduled for this afternoon. Knowing how you feel about poetry," she tacked on sweetly.

He surprised both of them by smiling at her. A slow, devastating grin that was not at all feigned. "I've always enjoyed Frost. Carry on, Ms Fairchild. I'll just take a seat in the back of the room."

As he lowered his tall body into one of the chairs, a pretty brunette at a neighboring desk looked as if she was going to faint from sheer bliss. Gazing up at him through seductively lowered lashes, she offered to share her textbook. Cole shook his head, silently rejecting her offer. She might be only seventeen, but Cole had an instinct for spotting trouble. And this girl represented much more than he cared to handle, even if he were into seducing young girls, which he definitely wasn't. Now the teacher, Cole mused as he turned his attention toward the front of the room, was another story altogether.

There was no point in lying to himself. He'd been attracted to Molly Fairchild from the moment she'd entered the hotel suite where he was interviewing prospective teachers for the school he'd worked so hard to establish, the project many in the community had dubbed "Murdock's Folly."

If he'd thought building the school had been difficult, staffing it had been bone-wearying as he'd crisscrossed the country, meeting people who had answered his flurry of advertisements in professional teaching journals and newspapers. Despite their early interest, many walked out when they heard the salary. Others, although tempted to try a new life-style, reluctantly decided that they couldn't give up the advantages of city life—the restaurants, museums, theaters—social lives that didn't revolve around the Grange Hall.

Molly had been a surprise. One glance at her elegant ivory linen suit and tasteful pearl earrings and Cole knew it was unlikely that this woman was going to leave the bustling, energetic city of Chicago for the solitude of Oregon cattle country. In one way, he was glad because he'd felt something stirring deep inside him that he had managed to keep under control for a very long time.

"You have to understand, Ms Fairchild," he had said, frowning to emphasize his point, "we're a small, isolated community with a population of 347. Things move at a slower pace than you're probably used to."

"I grew up in the hills of West Virginia, Mr. Murdock," she'd countered smoothly. "I'm well acquainted with life in a small town."

"Why did you come here to Chicago?"

"Northwestern was the only graduate school I applied to that was willing to give me a graduate assistant position. I needed the money, so I packed up and moved north. Besides," she said with a quick grin, "I'm sure you remember how it is when you're young: the big city represents glitter, excitement—Disneyland and Las Vegas all rolled up into one."

Her direct gaze met his. "I've enjoyed living in Chicago. Very much, as a matter of fact. But when I saw your advertisement, I realized I was ready for a change."

"Are you always this impulsive?" *Unreliable*, he marked down on a mental checklist.

She laughed at that. A smooth, silvery sound that rippled under his skin. "Now that's a trick question if I ever heard one," she accused. "If I say yes, you'll decide I'm too flaky to teach in your school. If I answer no, you'll politely tell me that you're looking for someone more flexible." Her eyes sparkled with good-natured humor. "Let's just say that I believe in following my instincts, okay?"

No. It was definitely not okay. Because if he was foolhardy enough to follow his instincts at this moment, he'd cancel his next appointment, pick Ms Fairchild up, carry her into the adjoining bedroom, rip off that proper little white suit and discover the passion he suspected was lurking inside.

His gaze flicked over her. "That's a very attractive suit."

"Isn't it?" she agreed amiably. "It's a terribly impractical color, I know. Especially in the city—all the dirt and grime—but I saw it in a window at Marshall Field and—"

"Followed your instincts."

"Exactly."

"Clothes like that would be even more impractical in a ranching community," he pointed out. "You'd be better off wearing jeans and a shirt."

"If you spent hours every day in high heels, Mr. Murdock, you'd realize that giving them up would not be a sacrifice."

Her brow furrowed as she gave him another of those direct looks. "Why do I get the feeling that you're trying to talk me out of this job?"

"Of course I'm not," he lied, rising abruptly. "Thank you for your time, Ms Fairchild. I'll be in touch with you sometime next week." Both of them noticed that Cole failed to extend his hand. What only he knew was that he didn't dare. If he so much as touched her, his rigid control might snap.

Nodding briefly, Molly managed a polite little smile. "I'll be looking forward to hearing from you."

There was absolutely no point in taking any chances, Cole had told himself as he placed her application in the discard stack. He was given a graphic lesson in the waywardness of best-laid plans that same night when he gave in to impulse. Calling her from the airport before boarding the plane to Minneapolis, he offered Molly the job. She had accepted immediately.

That had been six long months ago. Six months of sheer hell as he'd managed, with increasing effort, to keep their relationship on a totally professional level. Until yesterday. Until she'd stormed into his home and, without knowing it, changed the rules.

Molly continued writing the Robert Frost poem on the board, grateful for an excuse to escape Cole's steady dark gaze as she collected her thoughts. When he'd first appeared in the doorway, she had half expected him to fire her on the spot. She had certainly not planned on being stunned by a smile so devastating that it should have been declared illegal.

Then, as if that weren't enough, he'd professed a liking for poetry and had settled himself in the back of her classroom as if he had every right to be there. Which he did, she reluctantly acknowledged. But the idea didn't make her feel the slightest bit better.

Although he'd been the one to hire her, Molly and Cole knew very few personal details about each other; all their discussions had centered around her work at the school. Since his behavior during the interview had been brusque almost to the point of being rude, she was surprised to have been offered the job. When the months went by without his softening his initial stance, Molly had concluded that for some reason she could not quite discern, Cole simply didn't like her.

That idea had been reinforced from time to time, when she was enjoying herself, as she had at the Harvest Ball or the county Christmas party at the Grange Hall, and would suddenly feel Cole's dark eyes boring into her. When she'd get up the nerve to meet his steady gaze, his grim expression would be anything but encouraging. Although it took a major effort on her part, Molly assured herself that as long as he left her alone to teach her classes in peace, he could dislike her all he wanted.

But unfortunately, that determination hadn't stopped her from thinking about him far more often then she would have liked. The truth was that she found him rude, infuriating, and dammit, intriguing. There had been too many occasions when she was grading essays and his dark, scowling image would appear on the lined sheets of notebook paper. Invariably she would scowl back and tell herself that the vision was nothing but a product of overwork.

If she was able to control her thoughts of Cole during the day, the nights proved to be an entirely different matter. With increasing frequency the man would slip unbidden into her dreams in ways that were every bit as thrilling as they were disturbing. But even then Molly couldn't remember a time he had smiled at her. Until today. She had the uneasy feeling that after having received the full effect of that slow, dangerous smile, her dreams were going to become even more unsettling.

Talk about unsettling! Molly could feel his steady, intense stare directed at her back. Her ice-cold fingers clutched the chalk a little tighter. Closing her eyes briefly and taking a deep breath, she turned to face her class.

"All right," she said in what she was relieved was a steady voice, "who would like to tell us what Frost is saying in this poem?"

Molly wasn't surprised when her question was met by silence. She'd learned early in her teaching career that the appearance of an outside authority figure could turn an entire class into pillars of salt.

"'Two roads diverged in a wood, and I—/I took the one less traveled by'," she prompted. "Any ideas?" Nothing. Even Randy Lawson, her star pupil, remained steadfastly closemouthed.

As her gaze drifted hopefully over the classroom, her eyes met Cole's for a second. His expression was both understanding and apologetic, which for some strange reason only served to irritate Molly further.

"Okay," she said, perching on the edge of her desk, "let me try telling you a story." There was an almost imperceptible groan from the back of the room. "About a seventeen-year-old girl," she continued as if she hadn't heard the muffled complaint.

"This girl lived in West Virginia, but she could have come from anywhere. Even here. I think she probably had the same dreams all seventeen-year-old girls have. She wanted to fall in love. And she wanted someone to fall in love with her. If it happened to be the captain of the football team, that would have been even better."

A handful of girls giggled, and a few boys groaned in unison. But Cole couldn't help noticing that everyone in the room was leaning forward, hanging on Molly's every word.

"This girl had given a lot of thought to her life," Molly said quietly. "She was going to be the first in her family to finish high school. Then she'd marry her steady boyfriend, who was going to work in the mines after graduation, just like his daddy and his granddaddy had. They'd move into their own little love nest—oh, the mobile home wouldn't really be theirs; it'd be owned by the mining company—but they'd be by themselves. Without any adults to interfere in their lives."

There was a chorus of deeply felt, obviously envious sighs as Molly's audience considered the vast possibilities such a living arrangement, free from parents, would offer.

"They'd have children, of course. Two, maybe three. And she'd take care of them while her husband worked all day in the mines. The girl had already bought a bolt of blue-and-white gingham for curtains. She was going to make a wonderful home for her family." Cole suspected Molly's soft smile was directed inward. "Oh, yes, she had everything all planned."

"What happened?" someone asked.

"Nothing that seemed all that earth-shattering at the time. One of her teachers began talking to her about going to college."

"Instead of getting married?" a girl asked with obvious disdain. A small diamond, more of a chip than a proper stone, flashed on her left hand as she flicked her dark hair back over her shoulder. "Why would she wanna do that?"

Molly nodded. "Good point, Wendy. That was exactly what she wanted to know." In the slanting bars of afternoon sunlight her hair reminded Cole of winter wheat under a sparkling sun. When he found his fingers itching to touch it, he curled his hands into fists and forced his mind back to her story.

"Well," another girl inquired impatiently, "did she go or not?"

"It wasn't all that simple," Molly explained. "She tried to explain to her teacher that she didn't have any money to go to college. Even if she wanted to."

"Which she didn't, right?" Wendy cut in.

"Hey," one of the boys suddenly spoke up, "maybe she had better things to do with her life than getting married."

Wendy arched a dark brow. "Such as?"

"Like signing up with the Navy and sailing around the world. Or joining the Highway Patrol and arresting wanted felons. Or at least going on the rodeo circuit."

Wendy was definitely not buying the argument. "What would a girl want to do those things for?"

"Well, maybe not those exact things. But there's gotta be neater things than putting on the old ball and chain. Even for a girl." He looked at Molly, as if for confirmation.

"I'll be sure to tell Debbi you said that, Jim Henry," Wendy countered. "She'll be thrilled to hear that you want to go sailing off to Timbuktu instead of marrying her like you promised."

"You can't sail to Timbuktu," Randy Lawson broke in impatiently, "except by canoe up the Niger. It's in the desert. Now if you two don't mind, some of us would like to hear the rest of the story."

At the scattered applause Molly gave him a grateful smile before continuing. "The teacher argued that applying for a scholarship wouldn't be committing her to anything, so the girl filled out what must have been a thousand pieces of paper."

"And then?"

"And then she waited. And waited. In the meantime, she kept working at the local glass factory after school, putting away money to buy some furniture of her own for that mobile home. Just when she'd about given up on the idea of college altogether, the news came that she'd won a scholarship to a girls' school in Virginia."

"A girls' school?" Wendy complained. "Does that mean no boys?"

"Not on campus," Molly allowed, feeling the point of her story was getting bogged down in unnecessary details. "But there was a coeducational university only forty miles away."

Wendy's eyes widened. "Forty miles? I'd literally die if it was forty miles to the nearest boy. She didn't go, did she?"

"She didn't want to, at first. But her teacher kept after her until she finally agreed to try it for one year."

"What about her boyfriend?" Wendy was not about to give up.

Molly took her time to phrase her answer. "He was proud of her getting the scholarship." She remembered how excited Billy Joe had been for her. How he'd been the one to insist that she take advantage of the golden opportunity. "Since she was the first person, let alone the first girl, in the valley to even have a stab at going to college, he told her that she should give it a shot."

Molly realized her thoughts had begun to wander. She shook her head slightly to clear it. "Anyway, one year led to another. And another. Then during her junior year she had a professor who showed her that words have a beauty and a power all their own. By her senior year she realized that she wanted to share the excitement she'd found in the English language with others. So she moved to Illinois in order to attend graduate school at Northwestern University."

"Did she ever go home?"

Molly smiled. "No. She got a teaching job in Chicago for a few years. Then she found a new home. Right here."

"That girl was you?" Wendy shrieked.

"Boy, are you ever slow," Jim complained. "It's a good thing you don't want to go to college. No one'd ever give you a scholarship. Of course it's Ms Fairchild, dummy."

Wendy stuck out her tongue at him before proving that, whatever else, she definitely had a one-track mind. "What happened to your boyfriend?"

He'd known all along that our lives would drift apart, that once I'd gotten a taste of life outside the mountains, I'd never return home, Molly could have answered. "He married someone else," she said instead. "They have five children."

"Doesn't that bother you?"

"Why should it?" She looked around the room at the familiar faces with unmistakable fondness. "When I've got twenty-five."

"Ms Fairchild?"

"Yes, Randy?"

"That's what it's all about, isn't it?" he asked quietly. "Taking the less traveled road."

Molly could have wept with relief that her point had been understood. "Exactly."

She could feel Cole's steady eyes directed on her face but refused to look at him. Not when she knew him to be so against Randy leaving the ranch, even for the four years it would take the boy to get his degree. Fortunately, the bell rang, causing a flurry of activity as the students left the classroom.

"Don't forget, there'll be a quiz tomorrow," Molly called after them. "Be prepared to recognize quotations from works by e.e. cummings, Archibald

MacLeish, Emily Dickinson, Frost and T.S. Eliot. Also, outlines for your term papers are due along with a proposed bibliography.... Randy, are you going to be able to make it tonight?"

She hadn't minded filling in for him at dress rehearsal, but the idea of playing Cassio in fatigues before the audience at the Grange was less than appealing.

"Don't worry, Ms Fairchild," Randy promised, "I won't let you down."

The boy thrust out his jaw, as if already anticipating the argument he knew he'd get at home. The defiant look reminded Cole of another young man stubbornly standing up to his own father. Although it seemed like yesterday, some rapid calculation told him it had been seventeen long years since he'd first dared to face down Garrett Murdock.

"You're as good as I knew you'd be," he said, once they were alone in the classroom.

As Cole approached, Molly busied herself clearing her desk. "I'm pleased you're satisfied," she said briskly, "since it's a little late in the year to decide you've made a mistake." She looked up at him curiously. "And now that I've brought it up, why has it taken you so long to make an appearance in my classroom?"

He moved his wide shoulders in a casual shrug. "It wasn't that I was ignoring the school. I've had reports of your considerable expertise. Not to mention all those times you've conned me into approving yet another one of your schemes. Like the Shakespearean theater group. And the literary magazine."

"Shakespeare was meant to be spoken," Molly stated firmly, repeating her original argument, "not read silently from some thick, boring textbook. As for the magazine, we had orders for the last issue from all over the county. In fact, we came within two dollars of actually making a profit."

"I know. I bought one myself." Sunlight was tangled in her hair, making the strands gleam like polished silk. Once again he was struck by an urge to touch her. Instead, he shoved his hands into his back pockets. "Still, as good as I knew you were, it's edifying to watch you in action. You had those kids eating out of your hand."

"I learned long ago that kids learn better if they can relate things to their own lives."

"Like *Othello* in battle fatigues."

She smiled at that. "You got it."

His dark eyes began a slow, leisurely tour of her body, from the top of her honey-blond head, over her long-sleeved peach cotton blouse and down her legs, which were clad in a pair of dark indigo jeans. At other schools she might have been wearing a proper dress, or even a suit, like the one she'd worn to her interview last summer. He'd advised her to purchase those jeans. But as he recalled what her slender legs had looked like in that slim skirt and high heels, Cole found himself wishing he hadn't been quite so eager to help her bridge the cultural gap.

"The play's tonight, isn't it?" he asked, returning his gaze to her face.

Molly imagined she could feel the heat as his eyes drifted down to her lips. "That's right."

"What time do you have to be there?"

"It starts at six-thirty." Although it might be an early opening curtain by city standards, this was, first and foremost, a ranching community. Work began before dawn, which made for early bedtimes.

"I asked what time you had to be there."

"Me?" What on earth did he want to know that for?

He glanced around the deserted classroom. "Do you see anyone else around here?"

"I should be there by five-thirty, at the latest," she told him somewhat reluctantly, still uncertain about what he was getting at.

Cole glanced down at the serviceable, wide-banded watch he wore on his right wrist. "That'll give me just enough time."

"For what?"

For six long and very frustrating months Cole had kept his emotions on a tight rein as he had gone out of his way to avoid being alone with Molly. Today, driving into town precisely to see her, he had acknowledged to himself that all he'd managed to do was postpone the inevitable. Giving in to impulse, he ran his fingers down the side of her face.

"To order some temporary corral for next week's branding," he told her. "Then shower and shave before picking you up."

His fingers were rough and calloused. If Molly was stunned by how exciting they felt trailing down her skin, she was appalled by the way his bold, dark eyes made her blood run faster.

"No," she said, unaware that she was backing away from him until she found herself pressed against the chalkboard.

He reached out, cupping her shoulders with broad, strong palms that were more gentle than she expected. "I'm not certain I'm any more thrilled by this turn of events that you are, Molly Fairchild," he said soberly. "But the truth is that I haven't been able to get you out of my mind since the day I realized that I'd be crazy to hire you. And insane if I didn't."

His voice was low and gruff. Molly's mouth went dry. "I didn't want this." Her soft words sounded false, even to her own ears.

"Oh, no?" His smile held no warmth. "Then why did you come storming into my home yesterday like a cross between a brushfire and a hurricane?"

"I wanted to talk about Randy."

Cole ran his hands down her arms. "And we will," he agreed smoothly. "Later tonight. After the play."

Molly decided to try a different tack. "If you and I show up at the Grange together, people will talk."

"So?"

Molly told herself that she should have known Cole would have little use for the opinions of others. "What about Marlene Young?"

"What about her?"

The word around the county was that Cole Murdock's relations with the owner of the nearby ranch were a great deal more than neighborly. As much as Molly regretted listening to the gossipmongers, she couldn't help secretly speculating about the relationship.

"Won't she be expecting you to take her to the play?"

"Contrary to what you might have heard, Molly, I'm very much a free agent. Now how about it? You let me drive you to the play, and afterward I'll give you all the time you need to change my mind about Randy Lawson."

From the restless, almost angry emotion in his eyes Molly knew she was playing with fire by even thinking of giving in to Cole Murdock. Then she remembered the renewed resolve in Randy Lawson's youthful brown eyes. He was the most talented youngster she'd come across in four years of teaching and Molly hadn't a doubt she could go forty more years without meeting a student with a quarter of Randy's potential. If it would help convince his father to see the light, she'd go to the play with the devil himself.

"All right, Cole. I'll go with you," she agreed softly.

Although Cole had suspected from the beginning that Molly wouldn't be able to resist using any and all of the weapons in her feminine arsenal, he was vaguely disappointed that she had agreed so readily.

Yet he shouldn't be so surprised, he reminded himself. She was, after all, a woman, accustomed to playing these little games in order to get her own way. Why should he have expected her to be any different?

What the hell, he considered. A night in his bed in exchange for his trying to convince Matthew Lawson that he could very well have the next Hemingway living under his roof. It was a fair deal. It would also allow him to satisfy his nagging hunger for the woman and get on with his life.

"I'll pick you up around five."

"Fine." Molly looked up into his shuttered face as if seeking the reason for his suddenly cold manner. She forced a conciliatory smile. "This is very nice of you, Cole. But I should warn you ahead of time that I have every intention of pulling out all the stops." The smile moved to her eyes. "I've been told that I can be very persuasive, when I want something badly enough." Actually, Billy Joe had always accused her of being able to wear away a stone, but there was no point in bringing that up right now, Molly decided.

Her eyes, wide and guileless, reminded him of a newborn calf's. If he didn't know better, he might have actually fallen for that Little Miss Innocent act. "I've not a single doubt of that, Ms Fairchild," he said gruffly.

With that he was gone, leaving Molly to wonder what on earth she had gotten herself into.

3

As MOLLY DRESSED for the play that afternoon, she dithered uncharacteristically over her choice of clothing. Since this was the first time her high-school theater group would perform for the community, she'd planned to dress up. Not that a sweater and skirt would be considered formal attire in Chicago, but here in cattle country the outfit would definitely garner attention.

She was already going to do that by showing up in public with Cole Murdock. All she needed was for people—Cole especially—to think she'd made the extra effort for him.

In the end she compromised, topping jeans with a pink cashmere sweater. She no longer cared that the seed pearls on the sweater might be considered odd with denim. If there was one thing she'd learned since moving out West, it was that independence and originality were not only accepted, but also that such traits were admired.

She supposed that was what made Cole Murdock the unofficial king of this closed community. He was unquestionably independent, and although he'd caused her to spend more than a few sleepless nights since her arrival in the county, Molly had to admit that the man was also one of a kind.

When she heard Cole's Blazer pull up in front of the house, Molly was grateful that neither Mike Baker nor Barbara Sheridan were at home. She didn't want to have to explain his unexpected presence, even if the reason for it was entirely innocent.

Pulling the lace curtain aside, she watched Cole get out of the Blazer and come to the door. Years of digging post holes, lifting bales of hay, wrestling calves down in holding pens and gentling iron-jawed horses had definitely left their mark. His shoulders were broad, his torso firm and hard as it narrowed to a trim waist. His hips were lean, his legs long, the taut muscles visible even through the denim of his jeans as he walked toward the door in a smooth, loose-limbed stride. He exuded self-assurance mingled with just enough arrogance to intrigue the most unwilling of women.

"Don't be a fool," Molly muttered as she checked her reflection one last time in the mirror.

Although she'd spent her teenage years wishing for curves that had never arrived, Molly had come to accept that the first adjective that invariably sprung to people's mind when they met her was healthy. At five foot four inches, she was neither tall and svelte nor charmingly petite. She was, she had long since decided, remarkably ordinary. Yet more than one man, seeing the wide range of emotions in her bright green eyes and the sweet curve of her upper lip when she smiled, which was easily and often, might have felt moved to argue with her overly conservative assessment.

"He doesn't even like you," she muttered. "The only reason he's meeting you tonight is to try to stop you from causing any more trouble at the Circle L."

Even as she assured herself that there was nothing personal in Cole's appearance here tonight, she couldn't quite erase the memory of those roughened fingertips trailing down her face. She pressed her palm experimentally against her cheek, as if she could still feel the heat. Her hands, as she slipped her comb into her purse, were anything but steady.

The doorbell chimed; Molly took a deep breath that should have calmed her but didn't. *It's nothing personal*, she reminded herself one last time as she went down the stairs to greet him.

Other than a grunt, which she took for a greeting of sorts, Cole didn't seem to have anything to say. But that was just dandy with Molly since she'd already begun to regret her decision to go with him this evening.

They were halfway to the Grange Hall when Cole's dark gaze flicked over her, lingering on the small handbag she held on her lap.

"You're an amazing woman, Molly Fairchild," he said, finally shattering the uncomfortable silence.

Although his words could be construed as a compliment, his tone held a harsh undertone of criticism. Molly's fingers tightened on the black leather bag. "Why do I get the feeling that I've just been insulted?"

"I've never met a woman who travels quite so lightly. Usually they come loaded down with blow driers, curling irons and enough makeup to paint the side of a barn."

She looked over at him curiously. His gaze was directed straight ahead, giving her a view of his strong, angular profile. His nose had been broken, which wasn't unusual in his profession, she supposed. Despite her unwillingness to display the slightest interest in the man, she'd learned soon after arriving in Strawberry that he wasn't the kind of individual to run the Double Diamond from behind his desk. Whenever there was work to be done, Cole Murdock could be found in the midst of it, and she had found herself reluctantly admiring him for not taking the easy way out. Molly had always been suspicious of things that came too easily. And the people who accepted them.

"For the record," she said, "my hair's naturally wavy. It drove me crazy for years when I attempted to force it into sleek, sophisticated twists and upsweeps." She didn't see any point in adding that the need for an air of sophistication had always been her husband's idea, not hers. "These days I don't bother to try. I don't wear much makeup, except for a little lipstick, and as for the hair drier, why on earth would I take one to the Grange?"

"I wasn't referring to the Grange. What about tomorrow morning?"

She was growing more confused by the moment. "Tomorrow morning?"

"I don't keep a ready supply of feminine paraphernalia around the Double Diamond."

"You've no idea how relieved I am to hear that, Cole, since eye shadow and blusher definitely isn't your style. But what does that have to do with me?"

The silence in the Blazer was suddenly deafening as Cole was forced to wonder if he could have misjudged the situation and Molly began to get the drift of the conversation.

"I can't believe you thought... You couldn't have... I wouldn't..."

She pressed both her hands against her temples, willing her pounding blood to slow down and let her think clearly. She couldn't have been more stunned or hurt if he'd suddenly slapped her face. "Let me out of here. Right now."

"Don't be a fool," Cole growled. "It'll be dark soon. Whatever else you may think of me, I'm not the kind of man to leave a woman alone on a country road."

"No, you're just the kind who thinks he should be repaid with sex for a simple favor," she spat back. An icy fury rose to overcome the pain his words had caused. When Cole didn't answer immediately, she glared over at him. "That was what you had planned, wasn't it?"

He shrugged. "You didn't exactly say no."

Molly stared at him. "You didn't exactly ask," she pointed out. "Are you going to stop or not?"

"I'm not."

He stepped on the gas, sending the speedometer needle past seventy, as if to emphasize his words. Cole knew he should feel like a damned fool for misinterpreting the situation, but all he could feel right now was relief mixed with a determination not to let Molly get away. Not quite yet.

She glared out the window, watching as the rolling pastures rimmed by gentle hills became draped in deep purple shadows. She loved this vast, open land more than she could ever have thought possible. Despite her anger at Cole Murdock, Molly knew she would always be grateful to him for bringing her here.

"Would you have?" he asked suddenly.

"Would I have what?"

"Spent the night. If I'd come right out and asked."

Molly was grateful that they'd finally reached the Grange Hall. Because she knew she would have jumped out of the Blazer at that minute, whatever the speed.

"I'd rather go skinny-dipping with a piranha."

She had slammed the door behind her before he could utter a word. As he watched her marching across the dirt parking lot, Cole realized that this was the second time in as many days that Molly Fairchild had had the last word. And as much as he admired her spunk, that much, at least, was going to have to change.

To Molly's vast relief, the play went off without a hitch. Unless, of course, she counted the youthful Desdemona's sneezing attack, which escalated into giggles as the Moor struggled to smother her with a pillow that was leaking enough feathers to make it appear to be snowing in Venice.

After a cautious start the audience had even joined in the action, greeting the Machiavellian Iago with hisses and boos each time he appeared on stage. Randy had been excellent in the role of Othello's honorable but foolish lieutenant; Molly was disappointed but not surprised when Matthew Lawson failed to attend his son's acting debut.

She'd accepted congratulations from everyone and was basking in a warm feeling of accomplishment when Cole suddenly appeared at her elbow. "Just when I think you can't do anything else to impress me, you pull off another trick," he said quietly.

She gave him a calm, level look. "You're overestimating yourself again, Mr. Murdock. Believe it or not, impressing you is not one of my life's ambitions. And they're not tricks." She turned away to refill her paper cup with the overly sweet punch provided by Barbara Sheridan's home-economics class.

"I'm beginning to believe that." Cole took the ladle from her. "Of course that's probably what makes them so intriguing. And potentially dangerous."

Molly shook her head in mute irritation as she reached once again for the ladle. "Watch it, Murdock," she said under her breath, "your Western hospitality is slipping."

He caught her outstretched hand in his. "You don't really want any more of that, do you? Let's get out of here."

Molly was about to tell Cole Murdock to go to hell when she realized that the low buzz of conversation in the hall had come to an abrupt halt. She lifted her blistering gaze from their joined hands to his shuttered dark eyes.

"What I want," she said under her breath, "is none of your damned business."

"What about what Randy wants?" he countered quietly. "I thought we'd agreed to go somewhere a bit more private and talk about it."

She hated him for throwing out the only lure she could not resist. "Remind me never to play poker with you."

A satisfied smile touched the corner of his lips. "Is that a yes?"

Before Molly got back into the Blazer with Cole, she wanted to get one thing straight. "It's a yes to conversation," she warned firmly. "That's all."

"That's enough. For now."

He grinned with blatant self-satisfaction and put his hand on her back as they walked to the door. The gaping crowd parted like the waters of the Red Sea, and Molly knew that by morning everyone within a fifty-mile radius would know that the schoolteacher had left the Grange with the county's most infamous cowboy. It reminded her so much of those old John Wayne or Glenn Ford movies she revered from her childhood that her exasperation melted away, and she couldn't help laughing as she climbed into the truck.

"You should do that more often," Cole said as her silvery laughter caused something dark and insistent to ripple just beneath his skin.

"I probably would, if you'd stop glaring at me every chance you get."

He stopped in the process of putting the key in the ignition. "I don't glare at you."

Everything else about Cole Murdock might have her coming undone, but with this, at least, Molly knew she was on firm ground. "Oh, yes, you do. And since we've brought it up, I'd like to take this opportunity to ask you to stop. I'm not used to having someone hate me for no apparent reason. It's very disconcerting."

From the catch in her voice, Cole decided that the hurt he'd caused her, albeit unintentionally, was genuine. "If I've made you uncomfortable, I apologize."

"I almost think you mean that."

"I never say anything I don't mean."

His words held an obvious warning. Molly nodded. "Neither do I."

He gave her a probing, speculative glance. "You know, I really am beginning to believe you," he murmured as he started the Blazer.

Molly told herself that he damned well should believe her. There was no reason for him to be so suspicious; if he'd bothered getting to know her, he would have discovered that she'd never been able to lie, not even to herself. She shouldn't be feeling such a flood of pleasing warmth at his almost reluctant admission. She shouldn't, Molly knew. But she was.

She didn't object when she realized he was taking her to the Double Diamond; the chances of carrying on an uninterrupted conversation in the town's only café would be nonexistent. And since both Mike and Barbara had made it to the play, as promised, the two teachers were undoubtedly back at the house by now, embroiled in one of their continual arguments. No, the ranch was the only logical choice, even though she would be at a decided disadvantage facing Cole down on his own turf.

Outside the Blazer the black ceiling of the sky twinkled with a million stars. Molly drew in a quick breath as a shooting star scratched its fire across the horizon. "It's so big, so beautiful," she said quietly. "You never see the stars in the city. Too many lights. And smog. But here—" her gesture encompassed the land and sky "—I don't think I'll ever get used to it." Her eyes gleamed with a light brighter than the most brilliant star as they settled on his face. "You're so very lucky, Cole. To have been born here."

Her tentative smile caused that increasingly familiar stir within him. The idea that she could revive feelings that he had successfully kept dormant all these years was disconcerting. As he pulled up outside the ranch house, he twisted the key, cutting the engine.

"What do you want?"

In the sudden silence his voice was rough but not cruel. If anything, Molly thought she detected a hint of vulnerability in it. Knowing Cole would hate her for commenting on it, she chose to treat his question lightly.

"I've already told you I want you to help me convince Matthew Lawson to allow Randy to go to college. And since you asked, I'd also love a sandwich," she said with a smile. "I was too nervous to even think about eating before the play."

His eyes narrowed to dark slits in the slanting moonlight. "I'll say this for you: you seem to be an amazingly easy woman to please, Molly Fairchild."

Earlier she would have taken his words to be an implied criticism. Now, however, Molly thought she heard a question in his tone.

"Yes," she said calmly, "I am."

His fingers toyed with a few locks of her moon-gilded hair. "Was that a true story? About your childhood?"

As his fingers brushed the nape of her neck, Molly wished she had the willpower to move away from his touch. "With a little editing for personal reasons." She hadn't seen any reason to include either the unfortunate circumstances of her birth or her disastrous marriage in the tale.

Her skin was every bit as soft as he'd imagined it to be during all those long, sleepless nights. "Was the part about the boyfriend true?"

Her full lips, which had been driving him crazy since the moment he'd first seen her, curved in a reminiscent smile. "Yes, that part was definitely true." Cole was seized by a dark jolt of jealousy toward Molly's unnamed lover. Then her next words caught his full attention. "Poor Billy Joe," she murmured, "I wonder if he's ever realized how lucky he was that I took that scholarship?"

"I can't see how he's the lucky one," Cole said truthfully, knowing that he would have been a great deal more selfish than poor old Billy Joe Whatever-his-name-was. If this woman had wanted to spend her life making love to him, having his babies, he damned well wouldn't have let her get away.

The light that had been shining in Molly's smiling gaze disappeared as a shadow moved across her green eyes. "Let's just say that while I do many things adequately, and some even quite well, if I do say so myself, I wasn't exactly a model wife."

At the mention of her marriage a gigantic fist began twisting his gut in two. "That's right, you were married, weren't you?" He'd know that all along, but for some reason he refused to explore, Cole hadn't liked to think about some faceless rival sharing Molly's bed.

"Yes. I was married."

"What happened?"

Ever since Cole's unexpected appearance in her classroom, Molly had been on an emotional roller coaster. She wasn't about to rehash her debacle of a marriage, not even to Cole Murdock. *Especially* not to Cole.

"It didn't work out."

"I take it you were married to someone other than that altruistic high-school sweetheart," he probed.

"That's right.... I thought we were here to talk about Randy." Her soft voice had an unmistakably firm tone that made him smile in spite of his annoyance.

"Do you know that when you use that tone, you remind me of Miss Haversham, my fifth-grade teacher?"

"I hope she was a horror."

"A dragon," he acknowledged with a faint nod. "The old battle-ax kept a list of infractions stapled to the wall. Five checks meant a note home to my father, which in turn meant a trip to the woodshed. Ten checks earned a parent-teacher conference. I couldn't sit straight in the saddle for days after that one. From then on I spent the rest of the year terrified of doing something, anything, that would earn any more black marks."

"Are you accusing sweet-tempered me of resembling this demon of discipline?"

"Only once in a while. When you lay down the law."

"Then I'd suggest you behave yourself, Cole Murdock," Molly said in a stern mimicry of Cole's childhood adversary. "If you know what's good for you."

"That's very good," he said admiringly. "I'd almost believe you know her."

"We all have a Miss Haversham in our past. Except in my case, it was Sister Maria Gabriel." She shook her head. "You wouldn't think anyone with such a lovely name could be such a demon with a willow switch, would you?"

"You went to Catholic school?"

"It wasn't exactly a school," she corrected quietly. "More like an orphanage."

Cole thought of his own childhood, growing up without his mother, and was inexplicably touched. "How old were you when your parents died?"

"Really, Cole," she insisted, "this doesn't have any bearing on Randy's problems." It wasn't that Molly was ashamed of her past; she just wasn't eager to share personal bits and pieces of her life with a man that she was so strongly drawn to, despite every vestige of common sense.

"Humor me."

"I thought you were going to feed me," she complained.

"I am. After you tell me about your family."

Her eyes were wide and eloquent in the moonlight as they searched his for reasons. "Why?"

"I don't know. Perhaps you simply piqued my curiosity with that story this afternoon. Or maybe it's because I'm trying to figure out why such a bright, intelligent woman who managed to struggle out of poverty and succeed in a big city like Chicago was willing to turn her back on all she'd accomplished to come to what is not exactly the jet-set capital of the Western world. Or," he murmured, taking her hand, "perhaps I'm trying to understand what it is about you that makes me spend too much of my time contemplating what it's going to be like when we make love."

His softly stated declaration should have shocked her, but it didn't. Not when she had spent too many of her own hours these past six months wondering precisely the same thing.

"You shouldn't waste your time contemplating something that isn't going to happen." Her pulse was beating rapidly. Molly wondered if Cole could feel it under his rough, stimulating fingertips.

He could. As he pressed his lips against the silky skin at the inside of her wrist, Cole detected the wild pounding of her blood. "And here I was beginning to believe that you were one of the few women in this world who didn't lie."

"I don't."

"Your heart's beating like a baby jackrabbit's."

"Of course it is. You're making me nervous."

His smile was warm, lazy and seductive. "Personally, I'd call it something a bit more elemental. But I'm willing to settle on nervous. Until one of us comes up with a better word."

She watched, unable to move as his head descended, his intent obvious. Part of her mind told her to back away—both physically and emotionally—before she got hurt. Another, more sensual part had been waiting too long for this kiss to reject it now.

Molly hadn't realized she'd been holding her breath until his lips touched hers and she released it in a soft, blissful sigh. As often as she had imagined this kiss, fantasized about it over the past six months, dreamed about it in the cold loneliness of her single bed, she had not expected such tenderness.

Cole Murdock was not a gentle man. This country called for strong, hard individuals, men not simply capable of meeting the vigorous tests nature threw up on an almost daily basis, but of thriving on the challenge of besting the unpredictable environment. But as his lips brushed teasingly, tantalizingly over hers, Molly closed her eyes and imagined butterflies flitting over a newly mown meadow. As a slow languor spread through her like melting rays of warm, golden light, a low moan escaped her.

The kiss may have been planned, but Cole's reaction could not have been. He wanted her. He'd wanted her for months. The raging hunger that the mere taste of her inspired was surprising in its strength, yet not entirely unexpected. But what Cole had not counted on, what he was stunned to be feeling, was a need so intense that it was physically painful.

It was one thing to want Molly more than he'd ever wanted another woman. But to need her so desperately smacked of weakness. And no one had ever dared accuse Cole Murdock of being a weak man.

He dragged his lips up her cheek, determined to break away while he was still able to resist the almost overwhelming pull. Then she murmured his name, not once but twice in a whispered tone that was a beguiling blend of feminine awe and womanly demand.

"Oh, again," she said, lifting her arms to run her fingers through the dark waves of his hair.

Wondering if he would ever be able to deny this woman anything again, Cole traced the outline of her top lip with the tip of his tongue. She tried to tell herself that she was being foolhardy, that by allowing her heart and her body to rule her head she was displaying no more sense than the adolescent Wendy. But when his strong white teeth nipped ever so slightly at her bottom lip, something like the flutter of hummingbird wings stirred in her stomach and Molly ceased thinking.

Every nerve ending in her body was on edge, anticipating a fiery assault on her senses as her own desire escalated to previously unknown heights. But except for tilting his head to change the angle of the kiss, Cole seemed in no hurry to alter the leisurely pace.

He pressed his lips against her throat. She felt like satin and tasted like honey. Molly never wore fragrance; he'd noticed that the very first day when she'd entered the hotel suite smelling faintly of soap. The crisp, clean scent had lingered in his memory, enabling him to know, without looking around, the instant she walked into a room. It reminded him of dappled sunshine, of newly mown meadows, of clear blue skies and trees wearing their bright new leaves in springtime. Realizing that he was beginning to wax poetic—a definite first for him—Cole laughed softly as he nuzzled her neck.

Molly tilted her head back, looking up at him curiously. "What's wrong?"

"Nothing. I was just thinking how great I feel." Unreasonably lighthearted, he ran his hands down her sides. "And how great you feel."

She smiled at that, although her eyes remained wary. "I feel like one of my kids. I can't remember the last time I made out in a truck."

He frowned as he looked around. "Damn. I don't know what I was thinking of, keeping you out here when we could have been sitting in front of a nice warm fire. Come on in and I'll fix you that sandwich," he promised. "Then you can decide what you want for dessert."

The sensual invitation was just lying there, waiting for her to pick up on it. "The sandwich sounds terrific. The fire, too," she admitted in a soft rush of words. "But I'm still not going to stay with you, Cole. I'm here to discuss Randy. That's all."

His long, silent study did nothing to instill calm, but Molly held his thoughtful gaze with a level one of her own. The silver moonlight, dancing through the trees surrounding the house, created ominous shadows on the harshly etched planes and hollows of his face, but his black eyes remained mild.

"Whatever you say," he agreed, picking up his hat, which her questing hands had knocked off. "There'll be other times."

"I don't think that would be a very good idea."

Cole's answering smile didn't quite reach his eyes. "Neither do I. But I don't think it's going to be that easy, Molly. Not any longer." He held out his hand to help her out of the truck. As his fingers curled around hers, Molly felt the warmth all the way to her toes.

No, she agreed silently, it probably wouldn't. Nothing about Cole Murdock had been the slightest bit easy, and if the past twenty-four hours were any indication, things could only get worse.

4

IT WASN'T THE FIRST TIME she had been in Cole's home. Besides her impromptu visit the day before, she had come here on business on several other occasions. But she had never been so aware of her surroundings as she was this evening.

The house, constructed of native wood and stone, celebrated the rugged beauty of its setting. The living room, den and kitchen were linked by what seemed to be miles of flagstone. Massive hand-hewn crossbeams spanned high, vaulted ceilings.

The furniture was oak, heavy and simply carved, the upholstered pieces covered in a soft leather the color of perfectly browned biscuits. Framed portraits of prize-winning bulls lined the walls, and Indian rugs woven in warm earth tones were scattered over the floor.

What she had seen of the house was meticulously clean; Molly speculated that she could run her finger along the top of the picture frames and not find a speck of dust. Still, there wasn't a doubt that it was a man's house. In her mind she couldn't resist placing an earthenware bowl filled with wildflowers on the thick oak table. A woolen throw would brighten up one corner of the sofa, and instead of heavy shutters at the windows, Molly would have chosen an oatmeal-hued monk's cloth. She smiled as she recalled the bolt of blue gingham left behind by that young woman so many years ago.

"Something funny?" Cole asked as they entered the kitchen.

Molly shook her head. "Not really. There's just something about your home that seems to invite memories."

"It's probably because it's so old." He pulled a thick red steak out of the refrigerator and began slicing it into strips. "My grandfather built it on the site of his original homestead cabin. As a matter of fact, he built it *around* the cabin so my grandmother wouldn't have to live in a tent during construction. After the walls and roof were up, he simply tore the old place down."

"That was ingenious."

Cole shrugged. "It was practical," he corrected as he opened a bottle of wine. "That's the first thing you learn in the cattle business. Practicality. Only the sensible men survive out here."

"Did you always want to be a rancher?" Molly asked, smiling her thanks as she accepted a glass of ruby merlot. It was smooth and surprisingly complex, not unlike the man who'd poured it.

"Probably," he answered as he turned on the range. Blue flames licked at the bottom of the heavy cast-iron skillet. "Of course, I was born into this job, so I never gave it a great deal of thought until after I left to go to college."

He stopped in the act of frying the sizzling beef to glance at her. "That's something you're going to have to understand if you're determined to take on Matt Lawson, Molly. There's very little practical opportunity for other employment unless a man's willing to leave the county. I'd guess you'd say we're all preordained to tend cattle and ride horses."

Molly ran her finger around the rim of her wineglass as she considered what he'd said. "But you left," she argued quietly.

"I left. But I came back. One of the problems I'm having with your latest idea is that I'm not at all certain that's what you want for Randy."

"I only want what's best for him."

"Do you? Or do you simply want an opportunity to reenact that heartwarming little homily you told your class this afternoon? The one about the dedicated, noble teacher helping the impoverished kid escape a dead-end future."

"It was different for me," Molly insisted. "In the first place, Randy is far from impoverished. I grew up in a rough part of the country."

Cole's tone became challenging. "You don't think Randy knows about rough? He's been working alongside Matt since he was five years old. Hell, he won his first belt buckle at nine."

Molly knew that was a badge of honor of sorts. No cowboy worth his salt would ever buy a buckle; won in rodeo events, they were like war medals, displayed proudly on hand-tooled leather belts.

"Randy knows about hard work," she admitted. "But this place—" she waved her hand, encompassing the entire county "—is like Sunnybrook Farm compared to where I grew up. In fact, my home's major claim to fame is the Hatfield family feud."

She'd successfully diverted his attention from his planned argument. "Hatfield? As in Hatfield and Mc-Coy?"

"My maternal grandmother was a Hatfield. I remember hearing that her daddy carried two pistols: one in the right front pocket and one in his hip pocket. That way, if anyone got his right hand, he'd be able to get them with his left."

"Sounds like my grandfather could've used your great-grandfather's help during his battles with rustlers," Cole commented as he piled the beef onto thick slices of sourdough bread.

"From what I've heard about Great-grandpa Hatfield, he probably would've been the one rustling your grandfather's cattle," Molly said with a laugh. "There's a story about one Hatfield man who went out and killed seven men before breakfast."

"Only seven?"

"Seven. Then he returned home and ate seven eggs. One for each man."

Cole looked suitably impressed. "That undoubtedly explains your quicksilver temper. I suppose I should consider myself fortunate to get off with a lecture and a few cracked windows yesterday."

Molly could have died. "Cracked windows?" she asked weakly.

"Just kidding," he assured her with a grin as he held out the plate. "Your sandwich. As promised."

Molly stared at the huge pile of meat and bread. "I know I said I was hungry, but this is enough for an army."

"Hey, Hatfield blood or not, you're going to have to keep your strength up if you're going to scrap with Matt Lawson. Besides, most people around here consider Double Diamond beef just about the closest thing to heaven."

His tone invited comment. As Molly tasted the blissfully tender meat, she decided that most people were right. "Not bad."

He raised his eyebrows. "Is that all you have to say?"

"Careful, Murdock, or you might find yourself in the market for a new hat when that one starts getting too tight."

When he laughed, Molly allowed herself to grin. To her amazement, they talked easily for a long time about her work, his ranch, the play, the differences she'd found between rural West Virginia and rural Oregon. It seemed as if, after all these difficult months, she and Cole Murdock were actually becoming friends.

"At the risk of increasing your hat size, that was the best sandwich I've ever had," she told Cole some time later after he'd put her plate in the dishwasher and they'd moved into the den. "Who would have thought college curricula included courses on improving steak sandwiches."

"You sound a lot like the Double Diamond hands a few years ago."

"Was it hard? Coming back?"

Cole frowned. "It wasn't easy. But it was mostly my fault. I made some mistakes when I came home," he admitted almost sheepishly. "Mistakes that if you do talk Randy into going away to school—which, for the record, I agree that he should do—he's going to have to be careful to avoid."

Molly felt a renewed burst of enthusiasm at Cole's agreement to help her in her quest to further her star pupil's education. "What kind of mistakes?"

"I came back to the ranch using a lot of big words that I thought would impress everyone. Instead, I found out later that the hands were spending their evenings in the bunkhouse having a great old time imitating what they considered my high and mighty behavior."

He smiled—he was no longer hurt by the memory of passing the window and hearing his words tossed so carelessly and cruelly around. "I suppose I thought it was going to be easy because I was the boss's son. Instead, I discovered that made it all the harder."

"People around here say you've done a lot to improve the breed," she offered. "That must make you proud. It must have made your father proud."

"I don't know. My father and I always seemed to be at cross-purposes. We had a lot of arguments when I was growing up. A great many of them centered on my wanting to go to Cal Poly."

"Your father didn't want you to go?"

"He felt a lot like Matt. The day I left, Dad warned me that if I insisted on running off to California, I'd be giving up my birthright. That I'd no longer be his son. Then he pulled out all the stops by threatening to change his will to leave the Double Diamond to someone who'd have the good sense to appreciate it."

Molly experienced a stab of guilt for having accused Cole of not understanding Randy's dilemma when it appeared that he understood it all too well. "He obviously changed his mind."

Cole's grin was quick. "You Hatfields aren't the only ones renowned for having tempers. The difference is that ours are more like flash fires. I think the old man had probably cooled off before I got to the main road."

His smile faded as he recalled those days. "It still wasn't easy. The month I got my master's in animal science, Dad had a stroke that left him with some memory loss and paralysis on his left side. I took over the day-to-day running of the ranch, and although he lived for another five years, he never seemed able to come up with the words to tell me I was doing a good job."

Moved that Cole was sharing such an intimate glimpse of his life with her, Molly touched his broad, tanned hand with hers. "I'm sorry."

His eyes remained thoughtful as he linked their fingers. "I never really minded. That's just the way he was. I do regret that I never knew how to tell him *he'd* done a good job."

His thumb absently brushed the soft skin of her palm. "I'm not afraid to make mistakes, Molly, but I've always prided myself on being a man who learns from them," he said so quietly that Molly wasn't certain whether Cole was talking to her or to himself. "If I ever have a child of my own, I hope to hell I'll have learned something about being a father by having made so many mistakes as a son."

Since Molly didn't know how to answer that intensely personal statement, she remained silent.

Cole was surprised and more than a little uncomfortable to realize that he'd given Molly so many insights into what made him tick. Part of his reason for bringing her here tonight had been to delve under her attractive exterior and learn more about what made *her* tick. He'd already determined that he was going to have her; now he wanted to ensure that there wouldn't be any unwelcome surprises later on. Such as the possibility that Molly was angling for that home she'd given up so many years ago. The one with the husband, kids and gingham curtains. Except for a few facts that he could have gleaned from her neatly typed resumé, he'd discovered little new about her. Instead, his damned runaway mouth had been on fast forward most of the night.

Uneasy with the situation and needing time to determine exactly how to put things back on course, Cole glanced pointedly at his watch. "It's getting late. Since you've turned down my offer of Double Diamond hospitality, I'd better take you home."

She checked her own watch, amazed to find that it was after midnight. As they walked to the truck, Molly was a little disappointed that Cole didn't use the opportunity to put his arm around her. After all, he had the perfect excuse. Although it might be spring according to the calendar, winter continued to linger in the night air. But she didn't say anything.

There wasn't much conversation on the drive back to Molly's house, but this time the silence seemed to be comfortably companionable rather than a tautly held truce. Leaning her head back against the seat, Molly closed her eyes and promptly fell asleep.

IT WAS THE FEATHERY TOUCH of his fingers stroking her lips that coaxed Molly back to consciousness. "I'm sorry."

Cole seemed transfixed by the way her lips parted instinctively at his touch. "Don't be. It's late. You had a long day." He smiled slowly. "I knew you should have stayed with me at the ranch."

"Am I supposed to believe that I would've gotten a lot of sleep there?"

"Not if I'd had anything to say about it," he admitted amiably. He trailed his hand down her throat, satisfied as he felt her pulse jump in response. "Did I tell you how much I like this sweater?" he asked as his hands brushed lightly, carelessly over the slope of her breasts.

Molly swallowed. "I don't think the subject came up."

"I must have been spending too much time around the bunkhouse. It appears that I've forgotten how to court a lovely lady properly." When his fingers traced the design of seed pearls across her collarbone, then skimmed lightly over her breasts, Molly's blood pounded warmly. "It's cashmere, isn't it?"

"Yes," she managed to say weakly. Molly knew that if Cole had touched her this way back in the cozy, rustic den of the Double Diamond, she never would have had the strength to leave.

He nodded. "I thought so. It reminds me of you. Soft, inviting."

"Cole—"

He bent his head, cutting off her soft protest as his mouth claimed hers. "There's a saying," he murmured, punctuating his words with light, teasing kisses, "that people around these parts are as tough as leather but as good as velvet." His hands deftly slipped under her sweater. "I don't know about the leather, but you definitely fit the velvet category, Molly Fairchild."

The words were smooth, practiced. "You were much too hard on yourself earlier, Cole," she said, slipping out of his embrace.

He frowned. "When was that?"

"When you apologized for your lack of courting expertise. Personally, I don't believe you've forgotten a thing."

So much for the tried-and-true, he thought wryly. "Do you know that I'm beginning to get the uncomfortable impression that you can see right through me?" he complained, resisting one last touch as he reluctantly straightened her sweater.

"Would that be so bad?"

"I don't like the idea of things being one-sided. You already know that I want you."

"I believe you've mentioned that fact."

"But you haven't said what you want from me."

"Why do I have to want something from you?" she argued heatedly, her irritation flaring at the way he kept perceiving her.

"Dammit, I learned a long time ago that all women want something. Why should you be any different?"

"I thought we'd determined that I'm not like other women."

His eyes narrowed. "If that's really true, sweetheart, then you're either awfully naive or more dangerous than I thought."

There it was again. That strangely bitter suspicion. Molly rubbed her temples wearily, unwilling to deal with it anymore that night.

"Look, Cole, it's late, I'm exhausted and I'm beginning to get a splitting headache. If it'll make you feel any better, I'll admit that this has all been one gigantic plot. I purposely wore this sweater tonight because I knew you'd never be able to resist it. I moved into a house with two other people six months ago so you'd be forced to take me to the ranch tonight, where I could ply you with your own wine until I had you fully in my feminine power. But why stop there?" she asked acidly, her voice rising. "If you want the unvarnished truth, I cleverly arranged for you to come to Chicago last year because I always wanted to teach at some cattle town in the middle of nowhere. It's so much easier to mess in people's private lives in small towns, don't you think?"

"Molly—"

She jerked her arm away, shaking off his placating hand as she flung open the passenger door. "See those stars out there?" she asked with a sweeping motion of her hand. "I arranged for them, Cole. Every last one. The moon, as well. All by myself, so the night would be more romantic when I used my wicked, womanly wiles to trick you into helping me with Matthew Lawson."

She jumped down to the sidewalk and glared up at him. In the amber glow from the streetlight her eyes reminded him of emerald fire. "How clever of you to see through my subterfuge; I guess that's what I get for underestimating a Murdock. Don't worry, Cole, I won't be bothering you again." She turned away.

Cole's next words, softly couched, stopped her in her tracks. "I'll pick you up Saturday. At noon."

She'd had a weekend ski trip to Timberline with Mike and Barbara planned for the past six weeks. She certainly wasn't going to give it up to fight with Cole all afternoon.

"I'm busy Saturday."

"I know. Having dinner with me. At the Double Diamond."

She wondered if he'd heard a word she'd said. "I'm not having dinner with you, Cole."

"Not with me alone," he agreed. "Matt's always been a sucker for Dallas's apple pie." He winked, slowly. "Not that you're not a damned desirable woman, but if you want to try to corral a man, Molly, especially Matt Lawson, you stand a lot better chance if you toss in a freshly baked, piping hot apple pie."

Molly stared at him, trying to understand this sudden turnaround. "I should just toss your offer to help right back in your smug face," she said finally.

"But you won't."

She smiled ruefully. "Of course I won't. Randy's too important. Noon. And don't bother picking me up. I know the way."

He didn't argue. "It's a date." He reached across the wide bench seat to pull closed the door she'd left open.

"A date," Molly echoed, wishing he'd chosen any other word. One that didn't carry undertones of intimacy. She turned away and walked up the steps of the old house, refusing to look back as she heard the Blazer pull away from the curb.

"WELL, IF IT ISN'T the Sultan of Software," Molly said as she entered the kitchen the following morning.

A tall, lanky man dressed in flowing robes and an orange turban turned from the range and gave her a deep bow. "PCing is believing," Mike Baker greeted her cheerfully.

"And the MacMeek shall inherit the earth," she answered Mike Baker's greeting absently as she stared at a platter piled with bacon. He must have fried at least five pounds already. And it wasn't even seven o'clock. "What army do you have hiding out in the bushes?"

As he followed her gaze, Mike grimaced. "I guess I did it again. I was thinking about a program and lost track." He held out the plate. "Want to help me out?"

"You'll need every man, woman and child in the county to even make a dent in this," she said as she plucked a piece of crisp bacon from the stack. "I take it you were up all night again."

"A bug caused Moby mayhem in the software I planned to use in my fifth-period class this afternoon, so I spent the night doing chip implantation surgery."

"Oh, God." Barbara Sheridan shut her eyes in brief disgust as she joined Mike and Molly in the kitchen. "Aren't you ever going to grow up?"

"I certainly hope not," Mike answered cheerfully as he continued to fry bacon. "By the way, you look megagorgeous today."

His bright blue eyes displayed masculine approval of Barbara's coral sweater and matching knit skirt. Cole had uncovered the curvaceous redhead in Minneapolis, and although Molly knew Barbara had been given the same advice concerning the practicality of casual wear, she continued to dress as if she were still working in the public relations department of General Mills, pushing the wonderful world of pancake mix to the press. She was also one of the few women in the county to wear eye shadow during the day.

The striking combination of dress and makeup, along with an aura of extreme self-confidence, caused most of the local men to treat her in much the same way they might treat Kathleen Turner in the impossible event the movie queen ever came to town. They stared. A lot. But none of them ever seemed to get up the nerve to talk to her. In that respect, too, Mike Baker was unique. If the math teacher was at all intimidated by Barbara, he failed to show it.

To Molly's amazement, Barbara appeared momentarily nonplussed at Mike's compliment. She recovered quickly. "And you look ridiculous in that Halloween costume. As usual."

"Spoken like a true computerphobe," Mike returned easily.

"Can't you two at least wait until I've had my coffee to start bickering?" Molly complained.

It had been like this ever since Mike and Barbara had moved in, within hours of each other, at the beginning of the term. It was particularly bad on Fridays when Mike put on his Sultan of Software outfit and turned his classroom into a hacker's paradise.

Although Mike Baker's methods were admittedly unorthodox—he'd been fired from five schools in six years for his inability to maintain discipline in the classroom—Molly knew that the twenty-eight-year-old man was a dedicated professional. While eastern Oregon might not be the hub of the universe, Mike insisted that all his students needed to become computer literate in order to survive in a rapidly changing world. "Bringing bytes to the boondocks" was how he referred to his zeal in spreading the gospel of computer literacy.

"You know, if you got to know Gertie, you'd probably like her," he suggested to Barbara as he turned the strips of sizzling bacon.

"In the first place, let me tell you once again that I think it's sick the way you anthropomorphize that stupid machine," Barbara countered. "Besides, I have a theory of my own about computers."

"Oh?"

"They're nothing more than an expensive yuppie fad," she declared, tossing her head. "Just you wait and see, Michael Baker, your precious Gertie will end up in the archives of the Smithsonian right along with the hula hoop and Captain Midnight decoder rings."

With his unflappable good humor Mike continued to ignore her sarcasm. "Gertie could help you organize your classes," he said offhandedly. The Sultan had just said the magic word; if there was one thing Barbara excelled at, it was organization.

"Pat that bacon with paper towels before you put it on the plate," Barbara instructed briskly. "And for your information, I'm already organized. What makes you think that stupid machine of yours could do any better?"

"Shh, don't let Gertie hear you call her a stupid machine," he instructed in a stage whisper. "She's very sensitive."

"And you're crazy."

He shrugged as he held out the platter, offering her a piece of bacon. "That's what they say. Just think about it, okay?"

Barbara looked at him suspiciously. "Perhaps."

He grinned, apparently satisfied. For now. "Great."

"So," Barbara said as she poured a cup of coffee and sat down at the table across from Molly, "how did you and the Marlboro Man get along last night? It was clever the way you managed to scoop him right out from under all those women's noses. When you two started to leave together, Marlene Young looked tempted to toss a lasso around his shoulders and yank him back into the room."

"If you're talking about Cole Murdock—and I assume you are because everyone knows how Marlene is always making those stupid cow eyes at him—she's more than welcome to the man."

"Sure," Barbara agreed. "That's why you disappeared with him all night."

"Not all night. I was home before midnight," Molly said, fudging.

Mike joined the conversation. "One-thirty, but who's counting?"

"It was strictly business," Molly insisted.

Barbara eyed her over the rim of her cup. "And pigs have been flying all over the county." Her censorious blue eyes moved to the stove. "That must explain all the bacon—the Prince of PCs has obviously spent the morning shooting them down."

"I merely wanted Cole to talk to Matthew Lawson for me," Molly said firmly.

The teasing looks faded from their faces. "Is he going to do it?" Mike asked hopefully. "The kid really does deserve a chance."

"That's why I wanted an opportunity to talk to Cole alone," Molly said. "I went out to the ranch with him to try to convince him to see the light."

"And?"

"And I don't know how helpful it's going to be, but he is inviting both Randy's father and me to noon dinner tomorrow."

"So much for tomorrow's ski trip," Mike murmured regretfully.

"I know." Molly's voice had the same regret. "I was really looking forward to it, but you two'll have to go without me. This is my last chance. Cole's housekeeper is even baking Lawson's favorite apple pie."

"Good thinking." Barbara nodded approvingly. "The way to a man's heart is through his stomach."

Privately, Molly thought that Barbara was vastly oversimplifying matters since she doubted any man would waste time pondering the stunning redhead's culinary skills, which, like everything about Barbara Sheridan, were perfect. "Well, at this point, I'm willing to try anything. The last time I was out at the Circle L, Matthew Lawson threatened to sic his dogs on me if I didn't stop giving Randy crazy ideas."

"Well, whatever your alleged intentions, if Cole Murdock is going to be a regular guest around here, make sure you give me advance warning so I don't come downstairs with one of my mud masks on. Or my hair in curlers," Barbara instructed.

"I think you're kinda cute in curlers," Mike said.

"Encouraging words from someone who looks as if he's escaped from the audience of *Let's Make a Deal*," she returned crisply. "But what can you expect from a grown man who doesn't even own a suit?"

"Children, children. Could you please keep it down? I didn't get much sleep last night."

"If I'd been you, Molly, all alone with Cole Murdock out at his ranch, I would've gotten a lot less sleep."

Barbara bit off a piece of crisp bacon. "This isn't half-bad," she admitted reluctantly.

Mike bowed. "We aim to please."

"Then trash that stupid outfit," Barbara snapped before turning her attention back to Molly. "Really, Molly, weren't you even the slightest bit tempted? After all, the man's absolutely gorgeous."

"What is it about cowboys that makes intelligent, sensible women want to throw themselves in front of their damned horses?" Mike complained.

Barbara didn't miss a beat. "Their Stetsons are ever so much sexier than turbans. So, Molly, what are you going to do about him?"

"I'm not going to do anything. I told you, it's merely a business arrangement."

"That's why he's been looking at you as if he were starving and you were his own personal smorgasbord," Barbara countered.

Molly shook her head. "You're imagining things. If anything, Cole's spent the past six months glaring at me."

"Glaring?" Mike questioned thoughtfully. "I think you're off base with that one, Molly. I'm inclined to agree with Babs."

"The name is Barbara," she said coolly before returning her attention to Molly. "But, you see, even the whiz kid here has noticed. And he usually doesn't pay attention to anything that doesn't have disk drives and microchips."

"I pay attention to you," Mike pointed out amiably.

"I don't count."

"Why not?"

"That's enough!" Molly's chair scraped across the tile as she pushed herself away from the table and stood up. "Sorry, guys, but I still have some essays to grade before first period. You two will have to carry on without an audience." She escaped out the kitchen door.

"So speaking as another member of the feminine sex, what do you think?" Mike asked as they watched her leave.

Barbara's eyes narrowed as she considered his question. "I think," she said slowly, "that when Molly moves out to the Double Diamond, I get first dibs on her room."

5

MOLLY'S DAY WAS GOING exactly the way she liked—hectic and challenging—even though it had started with another argument between Mike and Barbara.

On Fridays the literary magazine staff met after school. In the beginning just a handful of students had answered her notice in the student bulletin and most of them had only shown up out of curiosity, declaring distaste for anything that remotely resembled literature.

When the word got out that not only was Ms Fairchild looking for original items to put in the magazine, but that she was also willing to look at word puzzles and limericks—although no one had yet gotten the nerve to try any really raunchy ones on the new teacher—the room began to fill with eager volunteers. Molly knew the *Clarion*, which is what the students had voted to name the magazine, would never garner any national awards, but if enthusiasm counted for anything, each and every issue was a winner.

She was lingering over photographs brought in by a shy girl who had never, in Molly's memory, opened her mouth in class. Karin Torgenson had always seemed more comfortable around horses than people. But Karin didn't need to talk, Molly realized, as she studied the stark black-and-white photographs because her pictures were worth all the words anyone would ever need.

Picture after picture told a story so vivid that no captions were necessary. The graceful arc of hurdlers at a regional high-school track meet was an arresting study of both power and beauty as the sinewy athletes appeared to defy gravity. In another photo square dancers whirled across a dance floor, the women's hooped skirts spinning like gingham pinwheels.

"Oh, this is the cover of the next issue," Molly said with a slight intake of breath as she reached the bottom of the stack. She recognized the scene as part of the rodeo that had culminated the fall roundup shortly after her arrival last September. This ride would last longer than the obligatory eight seconds: Karin had captured the blurred explosion of horseflesh and earth clods as a wide-eyed bronc burst from the gate. Thanks to her genius, the cowboy would stay on the bareback horse for eternity.

"These are amazing," Molly told the blushing girl. "I only wish that we had the funds for a photography course. And a qualified teacher." She tapped an unpolished fingernail on the table. "There must be a way," she mused aloud. "I know, I'll contact someone at Eastern Oregon State College. Surely we can arrange for you to take a correspondence course."

Karin looked as if Molly had just suggested that she fly to the moon for the weekend. "You're kidding."

As she saw the hope on the teenager's face, Molly remembered Cole's accusation that she was trying to recreate her own victories in her students. But Randy had a marvelous talent, she reminded herself firmly. So did Karin. If she could open new worlds to them, new possibilities, how could that be wrong? It wasn't, she decided. If she couldn't make a difference—even to one young person—she didn't want to be a teacher.

"I certainly am not. I met a man at that state educational conference last month who works in administration at the college. I'll call him first thing Monday morning." She glanced down at the photographs again. "Can you make me a few copies to send to him?"

"Sure."

Molly went through the photos one more time. "We'll want the bronc rider, of course, and the one with the cowboys silhouetted against the campfire, I think. And this one," she decided, selecting a candid shot of a smiling young girl, no more than four years old, holding a cowboy hat full of fluffy kittens.

"I'll have them ready tonight," Karin promised, throwing her arms around Molly. "Thank you, Ms Fairchild. I'll never forget you for this. Ever!"

Molly laughed. "Monday will be soon enough." She glanced up at the wall clock. "Shouldn't you be getting home? I don't want to antagonize your parents." Being in trouble with Randy's father was enough without Karin's parents getting upset, too, she thought.

"My parents think you're wonderful," Karin said in a rush of words. "We all think you're wonderful."

"And I think you're all wonderful, too." It was days like this that made the long hours and the low pay worthwhile.

MOLLY'S FEELING OF well-being lasted approximately twenty minutes. Inhaling the enticing aromas emanating from the kitchen when she got home, Molly decided that one advantage of living with a home-economics teacher was sampling the class project every Friday.

"You had a phone call," Barbara announced, turning from the range as Molly entered the kitchen. "From a man."

"He probably wanted to sell me magazines. Or a water softener."

"I don't think so." The other woman lifted a lid and stirred some spicy spaghetti sauce. "He said it was personal and to tell you that he'd call back later."

Molly's heart beat a little faster. "Was it Cole?" she asked with feigned casualness.

"Uh-uh. Damn." Barbara dabbed at some sauce that had spattered on her blouse. "I think he was calling long-distance. The line had that funny buzz in the background."

A familiar black cloud settled around Molly's shoulders. "I'd better take this stuff upstairs," she said, pointing to a stack of themes she'd brought home to grade over the weekend.

"Sure." Barbara continued dabbing at the bright red spots. "Dinner'll be in about ten minutes." As Molly left the room, Barbara's face mirrored her concern for her friend.

Upstairs, Molly didn't bother to conceal her relief when Billy Joe answered the phone on the first ring. "How is she? Is she all right?"

"Molly, honey, you've got to face facts," the deep voice on the other end of the phone chided carefully. "Your mama's led a rough life. She isn't going to be all right. Even on her good days."

"I know," Molly admitted with a sigh. "And you've no idea how much I appreciate your dropping everything to run up there."

"Hey, what's kin for, if not to help out in hard times?"

"We are hardly kin," Molly argued. "Considering that you're probably at least a thirty-second cousin." Neither Molly nor Billy Joe had ever been able to entirely untangle their complex family history. Part of the problem was that half the folks in the county where they grew up seemed to have the surname Pence.

"Kin's kin," Billy Joe insisted. "And besides, of all my cousins, you're definitely the prettiest. And the nicest. That should count for something. As for Loretta, you'll be glad to know that Johnny Cash's reputation is no longer in danger."

Relief washed over Molly. "She's forgotten all about it."

"You called that one right. When I arrived, she was sitting up in bed, peaceful as a lamb, watching *All My Children.*"

"Then she *is* all right."

"For Loretta," he agreed hesitantly. "Although she did try to warn me about some black-hearted vixen named Erica trying to break up my marriage."

"Erica's a character on her favorite soap opera."

Billy Joe chuckled. "That's a relief. Emma wouldn't take too kindly to some strange woman showing up at the house to steal away her husband. Not that there aren't a lot of days when she'd probably be glad to hand me over."

"Never," Molly admonished, a smile softening her voice. "How is Emma?"

"Just jim-dandy. She wanted me to ask when you're gonna come pay us a visit. You haven't met the youngest."

"How is the baby?"

"That little girl's got the strongest set of lungs in the county. I swear you can hear her all the way over to Affinity."

Molly could hear the pride in his voice, and for a moment she experienced a bittersweet stab of regret. Billy Joe and Emma Pence had managed to pull off what had to be one of life's greatest miracles: a family that knew how to laugh. And love.

"I can't wait to meet her. Tell Emma that I'll be back as soon as the term's over. If the school renews my contract, I want to talk to Dr. Wickes about the possibility of bringing Loretta out here."

"I don't know if that's such a good idea, Molly," Billy Joe warned. "Oregon's a long way from West Virginia."

"Don't you think I know that?" Her temper flared. "Don't you know I can't stand being stuck out here worrying all the time about what she's going to do next? Always counting on you to take care of my problems for me? I'm surprised Emma doesn't hate me, since you have to run up to Charleston so often on my account."

"Emma feels the same way I do. Kin's—"

"Kin. I know. But the fact remains that I'm damned tired of feeling guilty, Billy Joe."

"You've nothing to feel guilty about, Molly, love." Her cousin's voice was serious.

He didn't understand. But how could he, Molly asked herself, when even she couldn't untangle her confused and often convoluted feelings about her mother.

"I've got to run, Billy Joe," she said, uncomfortable with the way the conversation was headed. "Thanks again. For everything."

"Don't mention it. Oh, there's one more thing."

She was almost afraid to ask. "Yes?"

"Emma wants to know if you've taken up with one of those good-looking Oregon cowboys."

Molly laughed in spite of her discomfiture. "Tell Emma that her imagination's getting as wild as Loretta's."

"I'll tell her," he agreed with a deep chuckle. "And Molly?"

"Yes?"

"It wouldn't be such a bad idea, you know," he advised her gently.

"What?"

"You getting hitched to some guy out there."

"Just because you and Emma have the perfect marriage doesn't mean they're all made in heaven," she argued from experience. "Besides, I'm happy just the way I am, okay?"

"Okay," he said disbelievingly. "Y'all take care now. And don't worry about your mama. Everything's going to be all right."

Well, that was definitely an overstatement, Molly knew as she hung up. But at least, thanks to Billy Joe and Dr. Wickes, the current crisis seemed to have passed. Yet as relieved as she was, Molly couldn't help wondering how long it would be before the next one.

COLE KNEW THAT SOMETHING was wrong the minute Molly walked in the door the following day. Her complexion had always been fair. But today it was too pale, reminding him of alabaster instead of cream. There were blue smudges under her eyes, and they lacked their usual sparkle. At first he decided that her distress was due to her impending confrontation with Matthew Lawson, but her behavior during the meal changed his mind. Cole couldn't remember admiring a woman more than he did Molly as she refused to let Lawson intimidate her.

"Lori tells me that you've been shopping for a piano," Molly said as she passed a large bowl of mashed potatoes to Matt. Lori was in Molly's freshman literature class. Everyone in the county knew that the gruff, outspoken man adored his only daughter.

"Damn fool idea," the older man complained as he piled potatoes on his plate. "When I asked her how she expected to learn to play the dang thing, she dragged me into town and showed me this store where they give you free lessons with every piano or organ they sell."

"Sounds as if she's thought it all out," Molly murmured. She passed him the gravy.

Matthew grunted as he drowned everything on his plate—the roast, the potatoes, the peas and the rolls—in the rich dark sauce. "I still say it's a damn fool idea."

"Try telling that to Lori," Cole suggested.

"I did. I also told that fool of a piano salesman that there ain't nothin' on God's green earth worth a thousand dollars that can't have a calf."

"Right before you wrote out the check," Cole guessed.

Matthew allowed a sheepish grin to cross his face as he shrugged his massive shoulders. For his age—Molly guessed he was in his early fifties—he was still in incredible shape. Like so many of the older cattlemen, he carried his weight well above his trophy buckle. His torso might have thickened over the years, but his hips had remained lean.

"Women," Matthew muttered. "Can't live with 'em and can't live without 'em." He thirstily tossed back several swallows of iced tea as if he wished it were something stronger.

"Isn't that the truth," Cole murmured, giving Molly a wicked look she steadfastly ignored.

The conversation turned to ranching—the upcoming spring roundup, Cole's new Simmental bull, Lawson's Santa Gertrudis. Molly remained patient for as long as she could.

"I don't understand why you won't let Randy go to college," she said finally after the table had been cleared and they were lingering over coffee and dessert.

"I figgered Dallas's apple pie was gonna come with a pretty heavy price tag," Matthew commented. He scowled across the table at Cole. "Never thought I'd see you take the enemy's side, Cole."

"I'm on your side," Cole countered easily. "And Randy's."

"Then you're about as confused as a damned lost maverick." He stabbed his fork into the flaky crust. "Because the boy and I are on separate sides of the fence on this one." He glared briefly at Molly. "Come to think about it, we ain't seen eye to eye on anything since you got the bright idea to bring this schoolteacher to town." His acid tone made it clear exactly how much he thought of Cole's decision. "She's put it into Randy's head that he's got what it takes to be one of them damned writer fellas."

Molly counted to ten before answering. "Mr. Lawson," she said smoothly, "if you had listened to Randy, even for a moment, you would have known that he doesn't intend to major in English. He's a rancher. Like you. And your father before him. College isn't going to change that."

"Then what's the point of him going?"

"Your son has a love of words that's second only to his love of this land. You should be proud of him for wanting to explore that talent."

Matthew's expression was stony. "Give me one good reason why."

"Because he wants to write a history of your ranch."

As Matthew's jaw dropped, Cole lifted his glass to Molly in a silent salute that she acknowledged with an almost imperceptible tilt of her head.

"He wants to write about the Circle L?"

She calmly folded her hands on the table. Molly had spent too many years fishing West Virginia's rivers not to know when she'd hooked a big one. Now all she had to do was remain patient while she reeled him in.

"Your ranch has existed for more than a century," she answered slowly. "Unfortunately, with the exception of records of cattle sales and official things like that, the entire history of the Circle L, and the Lawson family, has been an oral one." As she leaned forward, Cole noticed that her eyes, for the first time since he'd seen her that day, had regained their emerald brightness.

"The old hands are dying, Mr. Lawson. Too many of the new men hire on for a while, then move here to the Double Diamond before drifting down to Colorado, Arizona and Texas. If someone doesn't record their stories soon, they'll disappear. Along with so many of the traditions that have made this part of the country—and the Circle L—great."

Matthew rubbed his chin. "I thought you said he wasn't going to go to college to learn to be a writer."

"He's going to learn to write," she corrected. "But he's always intended to major in animal science. Like Cole did," she added, hoping that the man could be reassured because although Cole had left home, he was back running the Double Diamond, where he belonged.

"I never went to college," Matthew pointed out stubbornly. "And I've done okay for myself. Some men don't need to go to school to understand animals."

Cole was curious about how Molly was going to handle this argument. If the growth of the West had depended upon men with college degrees to build it, they'd be having this discussion in Boston, Philadelphia or New York.

"You're absolutely right," she agreed. "And that's not why Randy's going to college."

"It isn't?"

"Of course not. But I suspect you knew all along that your son seems to have inherited the Lawson gift for knowing cattle."

"We've always had a knack," Matthew observed.

"But things are changing. More and more big businesses are getting into ranching, and by going to college, Randy will be meeting people who are in the same field. People he'll be doing business with for the rest of his life."

"I suppose you've got a point there," he admitted reluctantly.

"There's one more thing," she said.

"What's that?" He looked like a man who knew he'd been licked.

"You just told Cole that you're planning to lease some timberland from the Forest Service next year for summer grazing."

"Yeah. What about it?"

"You've probably already seen the forms."

He made a sound of sheer disgust. "The one thing the government does real good is figure out a way to use three pieces of paper when one would've done just fine."

"I know. Every year it gets harder and harder to figure my taxes. I can't imagine having to fill out the official paperwork for anything as complicated and important as grazing rights."

Knowing exactly what she was up to, Cole had to bite back a laugh as he watched Matthew's face cloud at the thought of all the problems the federal government created in his life.

"They teach that now," she said after a significant pause.

"Teach what?"

"Oh, you know," she said with a casual wave of her hand, "all those federal forms, profit and loss statements, cash flow projections, feasibility studies to take to the bank when you're seeking operating capital.... And, of course, he'll work a lot with computers."

"I'm not much for computers," Matthew warned.

Molly smiled sympathetically. "None of us is," she agreed with a mental apology to Mike. "But you have to admit they have their usefulness. Such as when you're trying to figure out whether it would be more profitable operating as an individual proprietorship, or partnership, or even organizing under a Subchapter S corporation. They're great for comparing loan rates, not to mention comparing your ranch with the competition."

She'd just gained his full attention. "A computer can do that?" Matthew asked in disbelief. As he looked out over the Double Diamond pastures, Molly could practically see the wheels turning in his head.

One of the first things she had learned upon coming to Oregon was that the Circle L and the Double Diamond shared more than a common boundary line. They also shared a long history of often not-so-friendly rivalry. Old-timers maintained that Cole had been the first Murdock in a century to invite a Lawson into his home. Over the past ten years the two men had managed to overcome past grievances, choosing instead to concentrate on mutual interests. Still, when all was said and done, Molly knew that neither rancher had lost his competitive spirit.

"I don't know much about it," she apologized. "But I do recall reading that there are computer centers which can tell how a given ranch compares with others on a local, state or national level. I'm not certain how they do it."

"It's broken down into percentages," Cole offered.

She flashed him a smile. "Thank you for clarifying that, Cole. It sounds as if you use a computer."

"Wouldn't be without one," he said dryly, knowing full well that Molly had already done her research on that score.

"All right." Matthew threw his hands up in the air. "I'll think about the kid going to college. Now if you don't mind, I'd like to get out of here before the pair of you manage to con me out of my new bull." He held out his hand. "Miz Fairchild, it's been, uh, interesting."

"And I can't remember when I've enjoyed an afternoon more," she said with a smile as she shook his hand. "Thank you for hearing me out, Mr. Lawson. I know you'll make the right decision."

"I sure as hell hope so," he muttered.

"Small towns aren't necessarily for the young, Matt," Cole said. "They want action. Adventure. Later they can come home again. Like I did." He rose from the table. "You haven't seen Goliath yet, have you? Come on out, and I'll show you this year's champion."

"You're going to have to beat my Santa Gertrudis first," he argued as he walked with Cole toward the door. "The way Grand Slam goes after those cows makes me feel young again. Why just yesterday we brought in this pretty little Hereford and—" A scarlet flush rose into Matthew's face as he suddenly remembered Molly's presence. "Sorry, ma'am," he mumbled.

Molly managed to keep a straight face. "Don't think anything of it. We had animals in West Virginia, too, Mr. Lawson."

"Want to come along on the tour?" Cole asked.

"Thanks, but I think I'll pass."

Cole nodded. "Another time, then. I'll be back in just a few minutes. Make yourself at home."

"But—"

"We have something to discuss, Molly."

She met his insistent gaze with a level one of her own. "I'll be here."

He nodded in silent satisfaction, then left the room with Matthew.

6

As soon as she was alone, Molly sank into a chair, shut her eyes and pressed her fingers against her lids. She hadn't realized how nervous she'd been until Matthew Lawson left and she'd allowed herself to relax. Two nights with little sleep hadn't helped much, either.

"Headache?" a solicitous voice asked.

Molly looked up at the smiling face. "I didn't hear you come in."

Dallas lifted a foot. "Moccasins," she explained. "At my age, aching feet settle for comfort over style every time. I'll be right back with some aspirin."

"Really, you don't have to bother." Molly's words were directed at the woman's back as she left the room. A moment later she was back.

"Here, take these," she instructed, holding out two white tablets and a glass of water.

"Thank you." Molly knew better than to argue. She'd gotten past the housekeeper on Wednesday, but even then she'd accepted that it was Dallas who had permitted her access to Cole's den. Rumor had it that there had never been a mule born in the entire county that possessed one-tenth of Dallas Cameron's stubbornness.

"That was a heck of a good job you pulled on old man Lawson," Dallas surprised Molly by saying. "I thought he was gonna choke on his pie when you told him about Randy wanting to write the history of the Circle L. Is it true?"

"Yes. I hadn't realized you were listening in."

"If a body didn't eavesdrop from time to time, how'd she ever know what was going on?" Dallas asked reasonably. "You ever think of doing a book about the Double Diamond?"

"No."

"You should. It's got a lot more interesting stories in its past than the Circle L. It's a better ranch, too."

"I'm sure it is," Molly agreed politely.

"Cole'd be happy to help you," Dallas offered.

"*Now* what are you getting me into?" Cole asked as he strode back into the room. "Last time you volunteered my help, I ended up facing the business end of a rustler's shotgun."

Molly was intrigued in spite of herself. "A real rustler? Like in the movies?"

Cole shrugged. "Actually, this one was a scared nineteen-year-old kid who'd crammed a big bull calf into his Volkswagen. If it wasn't for the shotgun, it probably would've been funny."

"That big bull calf just happened to belong to my brother," Dallas retorted. "And he didn't find much at all to laugh about over it bein' stole." Her hands were splayed on her ample hips. "But he is mighty grateful to you for tracking that rascal down." She began gathering the dessert plates. "By the way, I don't want you arguing with Molly today, Cole Murdock, the girl's feelin' a mite peaked." She tossed the words back over her shoulder as she left the room, banging the door behind her.

"I thought you looked a little pale," he said, studying her thoughtfully as he sat down on the arm of her chair.

"It's just a headache."

He brushed her hair off her forehead. "Want to lie down?"

"It all depends. Is that a trick question?"

He chuckled appreciatively. "Did you ask Dallas to get you something for it?"

"Ask is not quite the word. It was more a case of Dallas demanding and me being too meek to argue."

"Dallas has that effect on everyone."

"Even you?"

"I've been scared to death of her since the day she caught me hiding the peas in my mashed potatoes."

Molly smiled. "I used to do that, too, when I was a kid."

He ran his thumb lazily down the side of her cheek. "It was last year. . . . You have the softest skin."

She'd started to laugh, but at Cole's sudden change in topic, the sound died in her throat. "Like velvet," she murmured, remembering the other night all too well.

He put his finger under her chin and lifted her gaze to his. "Uh-uh. Not velvet. You were right. That was a line."

"I thought so."

"Actually, it's one I haven't stooped to using since I was in my twenties, if you want to know the truth." His thumb traced the curve of her bottom lip. "All I can say in my defense is that I wanted you, Molly. More than I could remember ever wanting a woman. And if that desire made me careless of your feelings, I'm sorry."

The quietly stated words gave her more pleasure than she could have imagined. She reached up and pressed her palm against his face. She couldn't remember ever meeting a man as complex as Cole appeared to be. So many layers.

"Who, exactly, are you, Cole Murdock?" she asked softly.

"Just a man. I could ask you the same thing."

Molly was drowning in the swirling ebony depths of his eyes, but she couldn't have dragged her gaze away if she'd wanted to. Which she didn't think she did. "I'm just a woman."

"No." He ran his fingers through the thick honey waves of her hair, pulling it back from her face. "No," he repeated, studying her with an intent expression that made her throat go dry. "You're not just any woman. I haven't lived an easy life, Molly. Or a celibate one. But not one woman—not one—has ever made me burn the way you do."

As incredible as it sounded, Molly believed he was telling the truth. She didn't know whether she was thrilled . . . or terrified. "Perhaps you've been spending too much time around Goliath," she suggested with a faint smile.

"This isn't a laughing matter."

"I can see that. I'm sorry if you find my presence disturbing." In truth, Molly rather enjoyed knowing that Cole had been no more comfortable with their situation than she.

He released her to pace the floor, displaying as much agitation as she had three days earlier. "It's more than your presence. Hell, you don't even have to be around to mess up my mind. I'll be working out on the range or in the barns, or trying to get some paperwork done, and you'll come waltzing into my mind and everything else flies right out." He stopped just long enough to give her an accusing stare. "When you first walked into that Chicago hotel room, I felt as if I'd been kicked in the gut by a horse. And let me tell you, sweetheart, it felt like a damned Clydesdale. At least. Oh, I assured myself that it was only physical. That once I had a woman, any woman, I wouldn't be wanting . . . needing . . . you so badly."

She had to ask. "Did it work?"

The atmosphere in the room had turned torrid. Cole crossed the room to stand in front of her. "I don't know. I haven't wanted any other woman since that moment."

The impact of that statement was almost more than she could bear. The grim line of his jaw sent her a silent warning.

"But you still don't trust me," she said quietly. "Not completely."

Something flickered in his hot, hungry eyes. It could have been anger. Whatever it was, Cole had it under control before she could discern its meaning. "I want to."

Molly was on intimate terms with heartache. After her divorce she had thought she'd die. Hoped she would. But in the long run she had lived, proving that broken hearts were not fatal. Having learned that painful lesson, she didn't know if she had the strength to go through it again.

"There are a million reasons why this would be a mistake."

"A million and one," he agreed.

"We've avoided getting involved for this long."

"We should be able to make it another couple months."

"Eighty-four and a half days till the end of the term," Molly corrected faintly. Her heart was pounding at the base of her throat.

"You've counted."

She nodded.

"So have I." Had he moved? Or had she? Cole knew only that her softly parted lips were a mere breath away.

"It would be crazy," she whispered.

Because of the thunder roaring in his ears, Cole felt Molly's words rather than hearing them. They were warm and soft against his mouth. As he knew her skin would be.

"Insane." His mouth covered hers and reason fled.

His lips were hard and hungry; hers were soft and avid. His dark hands skimming over her body made her tremble and when he boldly inserted his knee between her thighs, a soft moan escaped her.

"I want to be there," he said raggedly, pressing his palm against the part of her body aching most for his touch. "I want to be inside you, Molly. We've waited so long I think I'll go mad if I can't make love to you today. Now."

When he pulled her against him, replacing his hand with the swelling proof of his need, Molly could feel the heat through the layers of denim they both wore. She'd never known that desire could be so overwhelming, so uncontrollable. Her head spinning, Molly couldn't think of a single reason to object as Cole swept her up into his arms and carried her out of the room.

Molly remembered belatedly. "Dallas."

"Has gone back to her own house." His boots clicked on the flagstones as he strode down the hallway. "I assured her we could rustle up our own supper." When they reached the bedroom, Cole carried her across the plank floor and placed her on the bed.

"I spent the better part of last night worrying that you'd pull something like this," she admitted softly. When he frowned, she reached up and linked her fingers around his neck. "And the better part of this morning worrying that you wouldn't."

The relieved chuckle turned into a slow, deep kiss as Cole lowered himself to the bed beside her. He unbuttoned her cotton blouse, one hand deftly unfastening her bra while the other never ceased its feathery caresses.

The exquisite pleasure was almost more than she could stand as he trailed his fingers slowly, tantalizingly, over her breasts, never stopping anywhere long enough for the sparks to turn to flame. The pads of his fingers were callused, creating an almost sinfully exciting friction against her satin skin. When he rolled her pink nipple between his work-roughened thumb and forefinger, she bit her bottom lip to keep from crying out.

"No." He bent his head and soothed her bruised lip with his tongue. "Don't hold anything back, sweetheart. Not from me." He turned his attention to the other breast, satisfied as its already taut nipple hardened even more under his touch.

Molly's eyes were wide and luminous, and ribbons of desire, like streams of flowing golden light, ran through her veins. She watched him take off her boots, then slide her jeans down her legs with an economy of movement that fascinated her. She wondered how he could remain so in control. He'd said he wanted her more than any other woman; how could he not be experiencing the same urgency that was clamoring inside her?

Wanting—no, *needing*—to test the cords of his steely self-restraint, Molly reached up to pull at the snaps on his shirt with a forwardness that at any other time would have shocked her.

"I want to touch you," she whispered.

She pushed the shirt off his shoulders and threw it across the room. It hit the bureau before fluttering to the floor like an indigo bird. Her palms fretted over his gleaming flesh, exploring the rippling muscles that shone like polished marble in the slanting rays of the afternoon sun. Molly trailed her fingernail along a white line that ran from his armpit nearly to his waist. When she pressed her soft, moist lips against the scar, she could feel his stomach muscles tense.

When had the tables suddenly turned? Cole wondered as he tried to focus on something, anything, besides his swollen, aching sex. When had Molly captured control?

"I've always enjoyed playing with fire," he growled as he pulled her hands off his body and pressed her down against the mattress. "But let's not put it out too fast."

He sat back on his haunches and drank in the sight of her. His bark-brown sheets provided an intriguing foil for skin that had the creamy hue of gardenias. A soft strawberry flush colored her breasts, and roses bloomed in her cheeks. Her hair, spread out on the pillow, resembled strands of spun gold.

"You are so beautiful," he murmured huskily. "Absolutely exquisite."

Although he'd told other women so before, Cole realized that he had never really meant it until now. His tumescent body was aching; he struggled to ignore it. His head was spinning with her scent; he shook it briefly to clear it. His hands, as they whisked away the final scrap of ivory nylon from her body, began to shake; he forced control into each rebellious finger.

There was the sound of metal hitting wood as he pulled his tooled leather belt through the loops and tossed it uncaringly onto the floor. When his hands moved to the metal button of his jeans, Molly covered them with her own.

"No," she whispered. "Let me."

Suddenly mad with desire to have him inside her, Molly pushed the layers of cotton and denim down over his lean, taut hips. His sex was dark, strong and fully aroused. Drawing in a deep breath, she reached out, unable to resist stroking its smooth, satin length. When her fingers closed around him, holding him as he needed to be held, Cole groaned and thrust his hand between them, plucking at her delicate folds, discovering warm, moist treasures, and she trembled.

His thumb continued to brush against the sweetest spot, creating a rising urgency that was almost painful. When the expanded moment ended, Molly turned her head, muffling her ragged cry against his throat. Fired by the force of her climax, Cole drove deeply into her once. Twice. Three times. Each thrust deeper, harder, hotter as he abdicated the last vestiges of control to the primitive forces of his body.

As he raced toward delirium, it flashed through Cole's mind that Molly had stolen more than his sanity. But before he could determine precisely what it was that he'd surrendered to her, he crested, and conscious thought dissolved in a blinding white heat.

His breathing was harsh, strained, as he tried to gain the strength to move away.

"Don't go," she whispered, sensing his intention. Her hands moved soothingly over his back. "Not quite yet."

"I'm not sure I'll ever be able to move again," he mumbled against her love-moistened skin. "You are definitely something else, lady."

"Really?"

"I haven't lost control like that since I was a teenager learning about sex from Betty Louise Whytal in the hayloft of her father's barn. Next time will be better," he promised.

"If I did something wrong, just tell me, Cole," Molly said softly. "I wanted so to please you."

Unable to believe what he'd heard, Cole raised himself onto his elbows and stared down at her. "You're joking."

She turned her head, but not before he'd seen her distress. "It's not exactly a joking matter," she said. "I know that I'm not an adequate lover, but if you'll just tell me what you want, I'll try my best. Really I will."

If her pale face hadn't been so serious, if her soft green gaze hadn't been misted with unshed tears, Cole would have thought she was pulling his leg.

"Sweetheart," he said carefully, "I think you have things a little confused. I'm the one who could have used a bit more finesse. Not you."

"Thank you, Cole," she said in a small, polite voice that was far more suited to afternoon tea at the palace than this musky, love-rumpled bed. "That's very nice of you to say."

She sounded so serious. And so sad. Brushing a few damp hairs off her forehead, he bent his head and pressed his lips against her temple. She tasted so very sweet. Was it actually possible that she didn't know how incredible she was?

"How many lovers have you had?" he asked quietly. Cole suspected he'd be able to count them on one hand.

"That's a rather personal question," she demurred faintly. Right now Molly was wishing desperately that she hadn't brought up the subject.

He ran his hand down her side, delighting in the feel of her skin against his fingertips as he traced her slender curves and hollows. "We've just been about as intimate as two people can get, Molly," he pointed out. "I'd say it's a bit late to be worrying about modesty."

"Really, Cole—"

"Two? Three?" She shook her head. "More than three?"

"All right," she answered, shaking loose to sit up and lean against the headboard. "Since you seem determined to dwell on my lack of experience, the sad truth is that I've made love to two men. Only two. And you are one of them."

As the sobering truth of her statement sank in, Cole felt a surge of anger at Molly's ex-husband so strong that it was all he could do not to put his fist through the nearest wall, wishing it were the bastard's face.

"What was his name?" he demanded gruffly.

His blistering gaze was decidedly unsettling. Molly tugged the rumpled brown sheets up to cover her breasts. "Who?"

"Your husband."

"Oh." She unconsciously twisted her hands together. "David. Why?"

He put his fingers under her chin, drawing her to him with only that gentle, coaxing touch. "Because," he murmured as he kissed her from one corner of her pliant pink lips to the other, "David is a jerk."

She surprised herself by laughing lightly. "I know."

He trailed his lips down her throat. "I figured you would. You're a smart lady." He pulled the sheet away to allow his mouth access to her breasts. "So how come you don't realize that you drive men crazy?"

She certainly knew *he* was driving *her* crazy. "Do I?"

His body was stirring with a fresh torrent of need. "Oh sweetheart, let me show you."

Murmuring soft, inarticulate words of love, Cole moved smoothly between her thighs. As the golden afternoon slipped gently away, he continued to love her with a tenderness he never would have imagined possible, bringing her to peak after exhilarating peak.

The sun was low in the sky when Cole suddenly said he had to get back to work. "Unfortunately, I can't run the Double Diamond from bed," he said apologetically as he buttoned his shirt. "Although you definitely give the idea a fresh appeal."

Although disappointed he was leaving, Molly decided to be a good sport. "I understand," she said with feigned calm as she began gathering her clothes. "I can be dressed in five minutes."

"Hey, you certainly don't have to get dressed on my account." When he ran his finger tantalizingly along her collarbone, Molly shivered at the sensual memory of that wickedly clever hand on her body.

"I'm getting dressed on my account so I won't be picked up for indecent exposure on the way home."

"Home?" He stopped in the act of buckling his belt.

"Home. You know, a two-story white frame structure with a Chinese elm in the front yard and a vegetable garden out in back. While it's admittedly not as grand as this one, it's home. At least until June."

His dark eyes narrowed. "I thought you'd be spending the night here."

Desire to do precisely that mingled with irritation that Cole had taken her surrender so much for granted. "What would I tell Mike and Barbara?"

"You're a grown woman, Molly, and they're not your parents. You're not obliged to explain a thing. Besides, I happen to know they're up at Timberline. I ran into them at the market this morning," he elaborated in response to her questioning look. "They said you'd originally planned to go with them. I'm sorry if I made you change your plans."

"Having a chance to talk to Matthew Lawson was worth it. By the way, I owe you for setting this afternoon's meeting up for me."

He shrugged. "You don't owe me a thing. I was telling the truth when I said I agreed with you, Molly. The boy's talented. I especially liked that essay where he described a cowboy as a John Henry with a lariat instead of a hammer."

She smiled at the memory of Randy Lawson's colorful prose. "He is, isn't he? And if he gets to go to college to hone those talents, he'll have you to thank."

"I only set the meeting up, Molly. You're the one who did such a good job of pitching the product. . . . Is Matthew Lawson the only reason you're not regretting missing the ski trip?"

At the obvious bid for a compliment several quick, clever answers came immediately to Molly's mind.

Until this afternoon their relationship had been defined by periods of exaggerated indifference, interrupted by arguments and sparks of sarcasm. It would have been simple for Molly to fall back on a sharp quip.

"You know it isn't," she said instead.

Something that resembled relief flickered in his watchful eyes. "So there isn't any reason for you not to spend the night, is there?"

There was one very major reason, she reminded herself, thinking of Loretta for the first time since Cole had carried her into his bedroom. What if her mother needed her? What if Loretta ran away and showed up at Billy Joe's again? He was used to her staying in touch during these upsetting interludes.

Molly's troubled mind swirled with a complex range of emotions. She was so very tempted to stay here with Cole, experiencing the sheer pleasure she'd found in his arms. That desire made her feel guilty for even contemplating turning her back—albeit only for one night—from her responsibility. The guilt that defined so much of her relationship with her mother in turn caused her to feel resentment. And anger.

It wasn't fair. Her mother had never lifted a finger for her. So why should she have to be constantly sacrificing her own life? Damn. It just wasn't fair, she repeated to herself furiously. But since when were people born with a written guarantee that life would ever be fair?

Cole watched the emotions move over Molly's face in stormy waves and wondered at their cause. "Molly?"

His soft tone broke into her turmoil. "I'm sorry. I'd like to stay, Cole. Really I would. But I have to go home. I have some phone calls to make."

"You can make them from here."

"They're long-distance."

"I believe the Double Diamond can afford a few charges on its telephone bill," he said dryly.

"I'd want to pay you back."

Cole looked inclined to argue, but then he glanced down at his watch. "The more time I hang around here arguing, the longer it'll be until I can get back. Do whatever you want about the bill. Just don't leave, okay?"

"All right."

His expression lightened considerably. "Good. There's an extra toothbrush in the medicine chest, shampoo in the shower, and you're welcome to use my razor on those gorgeous long legs anytime you want so long as I get to spread on the lather."

His words brought up their conversation on Thursday evening when he'd accused her of traveling light. "Sounds as if you're used to last-minute guests," she said with as much casualness as she could muster.

"The Double Diamond's pretty remote. It can be a real pain driving people home at three in the morning."

"I can imagine," she agreed dryly.

If he detected her sarcasm, which she doubted since his mind seemed to already be out the door ahead of him, Cole didn't comment on it. "I'll be back as soon as I can," he promised, bending to give her a quick, hard kiss. "Keep the bed warm." With that he was gone.

Molly told herself that she shouldn't be so disappointed by his perfunctory attitude. She was a grown woman, after all; she'd known what she was getting into. To expect a man like Cole Murdock to suddenly begin spouting poetry or pledging his undying love was ridiculous. And hoping that he'd declare her to be the only woman who'd shared this bed was a hopelessly romantic delusion. Speaking of delusions . . .

With a stifled sigh she picked up the telephone beside the bed and dialed the operator.

7

THE RADIO PLAYED SOFTLY in the background as Molly worked in the kitchen. Enticing aromas bubbled from copper-bottomed pots while corn bread baked to a golden brown in the eye-level oven. It had been a long time since she'd had a kitchen all to herself and Molly was enjoying every minute of it.

An alarm buzzed, signaling that it was time to take the corn bread out of the oven. Molly glanced up at the copper clock on the brick wall, wondering how much longer Cole would be. It had been dark for over an hour. Surely he wouldn't work much longer.

She had no way of knowing that Cole had finished his chores and was sitting outside the horse barn, smoking one of the cigarettes he'd bummed off his foreman and calling himself ten times a fool for letting Molly Fairchild get under his skin.

He'd known he was going to have her. It was probably only dumb luck that she was as qualified for her job as she was desirable because he wasn't certain he'd have turned her down, even if she hadn't known a dangling participle from a pronoun.

He'd wanted her and now, dammit, he'd had her. More than once. But every time he'd touched her, kissed her, felt the tremor of her body next to his, it had only made him want her more. Their encounter hadn't gone the way it was supposed to. It hadn't gone the way he'd intended when he had invited her to dinner, then sent Dallas home early.

He'd intended to help her with Lawson—that part was simple since he believed she was right—then take advantage of what he knew to be their mutual attraction and make love to her. Finally, his curiosity satisfied, his desire sated, he'd be able to get on with his life.

That had been his plan. Carefully conceived, expertly executed. But then she'd surprised him with that ridiculous statement about being an inferior lover, and instead of shrugging it off, he'd found himself wanting to spend the rest of his days proving that bastard of an ex-husband wrong. He hadn't expected her soft admission of inexperience any more than he'd expected to care so for her feelings.

He inhaled, pulling the strong, acrid smoke into his lungs. It tasted lousy. That had been one of the reasons he'd given the habit up more than two years ago with a minimum of effort. That he had found himself needing a cigarette after all this time was additional proof that Molly Fairchild was nothing but trouble. So why didn't he just go back to the house and tell her to go home where she belonged? Now, before things became even more complicated.

He looked up, as if seeking answers from the star-brightened sky. Somewhere in the hills a lonely coyote was pouring out its soul to the moonlit night while Willie Nelson belted out an exuberant chorus of "Whiskey River" on the bunkhouse radio. The few cowboys who hadn't driven into town this Saturday night were playing poker, and muffled curses, as colorful and unique as the men who uttered them, drifted out to him on the crisp spring air.

Muttering a particularly pungent curse of his own, Cole ground out the cigarette and walked back to the house.

"You're back just in time." Molly greeted him with a warm smile that tugged at something elemental inside of him. "I hope you're hungry."

An understatement if he'd ever heard one, Cole considered as his eyes skimmed over her. She'd commandeered one of his shirts; the faded denim hit her at midthigh, displaying the smooth, firm legs that he could still feel wrapped so eagerly around his hips. Her hair flowed over her shoulders like a rippling golden waterfall. The remembered passion in her eyes had him wanting her again at the same time the soft vulnerability he also saw in those jade depths stirred feelings far more dangerous than simple sexual desire. Tenderness, affection, compassion—all those unwelcome emotions smacked of weakness. And Cole Murdock had never considered himself a weak man.

"You didn't have to go to all this trouble," he said, dragging his gaze away from those dangerous, soft eyes to the table where a hammered copper tea canister filled with wildflowers served as a centerpiece. Wildflowers suited her, he decided. Roses were too ordinary, orchids too tame.

"I like to cook," she said easily. "Although I haven't had much opportunity lately, what with Barbara playing Captain Bligh in our kitchen. And then, of course, when I lived alone after my divorce . . ." She shrugged as her voice drifted off.

Cole washed his hands in the stainless steel kitchen sink. "You didn't bother to cook because it wasn't any fun eating by yourself."

She nodded. "Exactly. So this is a real treat. I hope you like chili."

"Love it. Come here."

His voice, low and filled with passion, thrilled her. Unable to resist, she put down the long-handled wooden spoon and complied. "I was getting worried about you," she admitted breathlessly.

She had a smudge of flour on her cheek. He reached out and brushed it away. "There were a couple of breaks in the fence on the north boundary line and some cows got out." He wondered what secret feminine potions she used to make her skin so soft. It reminded him of the underside of buttercups. "Didn't want them dropping calves on Lawson's property. No point in tempting anyone."

"Surely you don't think Matthew Lawson would steal your cattle?"

"Not Matthew." His fingers trailed down the side of her face, under the smooth line of her jaw, down her throat. "But there's been more than one former hand who started his own spread with 'borrowed beef.'"

Her pulse was pounding so hard Molly could hear it ringing in her ears. "Speaking of beef," she murmured, "the chili's ready."

Cole reached out, turning the flame off under the pot. "Nice thing about chili," he said as he began unbuttoning the shirt, "is that it'll keep."

Molly grinned as she twined her arms around his neck. "I was hoping you'd say that."

That was the last either of them was to say for quite a while.

"TELL ME ABOUT your marriage."

Molly glanced up from spreading creamy butter on her crumbly yellow corn bread. "Why?"

"Because I can't understand how you could have possibly gotten the idea that you were unresponsive," he answered. "If you were any better, lady, I'd have to start collecting on my disability insurance."

Pleased at his words, she felt soft color suffuse her cheeks. "I'm not blushing," she insisted firmly.

"Of course you're not."

"It's this chili. I made it too hot."

"It's damned hot, all right," he agreed. "But tasty. Just like the lady who cooked it."

"Cole," she warned, feeling her body melt in response to his lazy, intimate gaze.

He grinned, satisfied, as the rose flush spread down to the skin displayed by his open-necked shirt, which she had put on again. "You are, without a doubt, every man's fantasy, Molly Fairchild."

"I'm almost afraid to ask."

"A lady in the classroom and a—"

"Never mind, I get the idea."

Despite the color that deepened in her cheeks with each of his remarks, Cole knew Molly was secretly delighted with his assessment of her lovemaking. "So what was David's excuse?"

"Excuse?"

"For failing to please you."

Momentarily stunned, Molly dropped her knife as she stared at him. She had never, either during those devastating months of her marriage, or afterward, looked at the problem with David in quite that way. Whenever she thought about making love with her husband—an act that had occurred as seldom as she could possibly manage it—Molly had invariably blamed herself for their obvious incompatibility in the bedroom.

"He didn't, did he?" Cole didn't need an answer. He had seen the wonder in her eyes when she'd climaxed, and he was glad to have been the first to put it there.

Her tone was amused. "Feeling rather smug, aren't we?"

He reached across the table, linking their hands. "I'd say we both have reason to be."

The mere touch of his lips brushing over her knuckles thrilled her. "You've surprised me," she admitted softly.

"Oh?"

"You were right about our initial attraction. Even though you gave me not one iota of encouragement, I've thought about you a lot, Cole. I fantasized making love with you more times than I care to count. And I always knew you'd be a marvelous lover—strong, experienced, powerful."

"If you're trying to inflate my ego, sweetheart, you're doing one terrific job." He turned their linked hands over and pressed a lingering kiss against the inside of Molly's wrist. "Don't let me stop you."

How did he possibly expect her to talk when her head was spinning? Her expression turned solemn. "But I didn't realize you could also be so tender. So caring. That was a distinct surprise."

Cole gave her a steady look. "To me, too."

Even as he said it, he expected the admission to make him feel uncomfortable. And it did. Immensely. But he hadn't counted on the vast enjoyment he received from the rush of pleasure in Molly's sober green eyes.

"So," he said easily, changing the subject back to its original track before he got in over his head, "what's the story with the professor?"

"How on earth did you know he was a professor?"

"Simple. For a moment while you were telling the kids that story the other day, and you mentioned the professor who showed you the magic in words, a sad little shadow moved across your eyes. The same shadow that showed up this afternoon when you said the bastard's name."

"David isn't a bastard," she answered automatically. Actually, she'd been the bastard in the marriage, as her husband had seen fit to point out on more than one occasion. A niggling little voice told Molly that this was the time to tell Cole about Loretta. She steadfastly ignored it.

"Isn't he?"

She shrugged slightly. "Perhaps. But the failure of our marriage was my fault as much as his."

Besides her obvious physical attributes, one of the things that had attracted Cole to Molly in the beginning was her spirit. If she had been at all intimidated by his power in the community, over the school, over her, she'd never shown it as she'd consistently fought for improvements she felt strongly about.

He'd heard a recent rumor that Matthew Lawson had threatened to sic his Rottweilers on her next time she set foot on his land. Apparently even that hadn't stopped her from fighting for Randy's chance to go to college. Her spirit, which Garrett Murdock would have called good old-fashioned spunk, was seemingly indomitable. That was all the more reason for Cole to hate her former husband's ability to make her doubt herself.

"He really laid it on thick, didn't he?" Cole asked angrily.

Molly struggled not to wince as his strong dark fingers tightened on hers. "Really, Cole—" she tugged at her hand "—do we have to talk about this?"

"Yes."

"Why?"

"I want to know everything about you, Molly."

"Why?" she repeated.

So I can sleep at night without thoughts of you haunting my mind. So I can work. So I can get on with my life. Instead, he said, "Let's just say I'm curious what makes an otherwise intelligent woman make such a stupid mistake."

His drawled sarcasm, so unlike the man who'd whispered soft, sensual endearments in her ear, was unreasonably infuriating. "I suppose you've never made a mistake?"

He looked down as he pulled a cigarette out of his shirt pocket. Striking a kitchen match on the underside of the table, he lit it. "I've made my share of mistakes."

Molly allowed herself to be sidetracked by the unfamiliar gesture. "You don't smoke."

He shrugged. "I know."

"Then put that ridiculous thing out before it kills you."

He eyed her through a haze of blue smoke. "Worried about me, Molly?"

She yanked the cigarette out of his fingers, got up from the table and drowned it under a stream of water from the faucet. "Do you happen to have any more of those on you?" she questioned archly, holding out her hand.

Cole wondered idly how many women could look so damned regal clad in nothing but a faded blue denim shirt. Class. Molly Fairchild definitely had it, he mused. That she had grown up hardscrabble poor in the hills of West Virginia only underlined the fact that there were some things money couldn't buy. Something his former wife would never learn, no matter how many hefty alimony checks she managed to accumulate during her lifetime.

"That was the last one," he said, lazily getting up from the table. "You know, a couple cigarettes aren't so bad when you consider that I could've gotten a plug of chewing tobacco from one of the hands."

"Yuck." She tossed the dripping butt into the wastebasket under the sink. "Don't expect any more kisses from me if you do," she warned.

He put his hands on the counter, effectively fencing her in. "You'd kiss me."

She tossed her head. "Not on a bet."

"Of course you would," he said patiently. "Because you can't resist my charms."

"Talk about egos. Of course I can resist you, Cole."

His gaze dropped consideringly to her mouth, lingering there for a long, silent moment. "Prove it." He took her face in his hands.

"This isn't going to work," she warned as his lips brushed hers.

"Give it some time," he advised. "I'm just getting started." His lips trailed up her cheek. "You always taste like sunshine."

"I thought it was velvet."

"I told you that was a line. This just happens to be the truth." His teeth caught her earlobe and tugged. "Sunshine," he repeated. "And fresh spring rain."

His warm breath against her neck made her want to melt into him. She wanted to taste him in turn, to cover his hard brown body with slow, moist kisses. She found every glorious male inch of him fascinating: his sinewy arms, his broad shoulders, his lean hips, strong thighs and muscular calves, those tawny nipples buried in ebony hair and how they'd turn to hard brown pebbles under her exploring lips.

She wanted to lie naked with him—under the stars, in a sunlit meadow, by a fireplace, in the old-fashioned claw-foot tub where he'd bathed her that afternoon. Molly was enthralled by Cole. And frightened by the way he could make her lose control with a simple touch or the lightest kiss.

His lips returned to torment her unbearably hot face, skimming over her closed eyelids, teasing at her temples, trailing down the slope of her nose.

"Damn you," she said with a soft, husky laugh, "you don't fight fair, Cole Murdock." Her hands thrust into his hair, holding his head still as she searched hungrily, desperately, for his mouth.

As her tongue darted between his lips, Cole's body hardened in response. "Neither do you, sweetheart," he groaned, pulling her unresistingly to the floor. "Neither do you."

"DO YOU THINK THIS IS WHAT all those glitzy novels call lust?" Molly asked a long time later. They'd moved back to Cole's bed. A few feet away a fire crackled in the stone fireplace that dominated the room.

He kissed the top of her head. "I suppose so." Actually, having had his share of lusty relationships over his thirty-five years, Cole knew what he and Molly had shared for the past several hours was infinitely superior. But he didn't know how to explain that without admitting to things that were far safer left unsaid.

She sighed happily as she cuddled up against him. "Well, whatever it is, it sure beats skiing."

He laughed and ruffled her hair. "I'm glad I've managed to live up to your expectations."

Her eyes, as she grinned up at him, danced with sensual humor. "Not only that, you've set a standard. One that's going to be very, very difficult for any other man to top."

Fury suddenly surged through him at the idea of any man touching Molly. Kissing her. Discovering that little mole on the back of her thigh. Loving her as she was meant to be loved. Cole Murdock had never been a jealous man. Until now. Until Molly.

It would have been impossible for Molly to have missed the sudden stiffening of his body. She looked up again, puzzled by the dark emotion she saw on his face. She pressed her hand against his chest. "Cole? Is anything the matter?"

He tried to remember when anyone had looked at him with such unselfish concern and came up blank. "I'm sorry, I was thinking about something."

"I hope it wasn't about me. You looked mad enough to chew a barrel of ten penny nails."

He wondered what it was about Molly that made him tell the truth when a vague, circumspect lie would have been easier. "I was thinking about you," he admitted roughly. "About how I hated the idea of any other man ever loving you this way."

Pleasure, pure and golden like a sunlit mountain stream, bubbled through her. She reached up, framing his scowling face with her palms. "I'm so glad. Because I think I'd want to horsewhip any woman who dared to come near you."

Her earnest expression made him smile. "You don't know how to use a horsewhip."

"Believe me, I'd learn.... You know," she murmured thoughtfully, "it's funny."

He pressed his lips against her firelit hair. "What's funny?"

Her expression became pensive as she stared into the flickering red-and-orange flames. "I never felt this way with David. Even when he was fooling around, I was hurt. But I was never as jealous as I think I'd be watching you with another woman."

"He made you watch?"

"Not like you're thinking," she corrected with a light laugh. "Good heavens, what kind of woman do you think I am?"

He had to kiss her. It had been too long since the last time. At least a minute. "I think you're one terrific woman."

She smiled against his mouth. "I think you're pretty terrific, too." Thoughtful again, she returned her gaze to the fire. "David never laughed. Do you know, I never realized people laughed when they made love."

"It's supposed to be fun. David sounds like more and more of a jerk. What did you ever see in the guy in the first place?"

"It was more what he saw in me," she said reflectively.

Callused fingertips brushed languorously over her breasts. "Now *that* I can understand."

He could feel her soft chuckle under his hand. "You've got a one-track mind."

"Yep." *It's stuck on you*, he wanted to add but didn't.

Tilting her head back, she studied him. "Of course, it's probably reasonable, considering your line of work." At his raised brow she elaborated. "All those bulls and cows making baby cows all the time would probably have an effect on anyone after a while." She grinned up at him. "I never realized that cattle ranching was such an erotic business."

"Neither did I. But now that you've brought it up, I'll be sure to take special notice." As he drew her more closely into his arms, Cole tried to remember a time he'd felt happier than he did at this minute and couldn't.

"I've decided that old David was not only a jerk, he was an idiot, as well," he said, returning their conversation to its earlier topic. His gaze caressed her face. Her eyes still held the lingering vestiges of passion. Her cheeks were a delicate shade of pink, and her soft lips were fuller and darker than usual. "A blind idiot."

"David was interested in my mind."

"So am I, remember? Who do you think hired you?"

Something occurred to Molly. Something decidedly unappealing. "Cole," she asked hesitantly, "you didn't hire me just because you wanted to sleep with me, did you?"

His answering laugh was deep and full. "Sweetheart, you've no idea how close I came to *not* hiring you for that exact reason."

"Really?" Finally, after all these months, she knew the reason for his brusque behavior. Molly was unreasonably happy to learn that he hadn't disliked her after all.

"Really." He lured her lips back to his. "So if David was interested in your mind, what were you interested in?"

Good question. And one she'd asked herself a million times. "I think I was enticed by what he could make of me," she admitted carefully. "David had a knack for making even the most mundane prose sound like poetry. And what he could do with poetry was sheer magic. The first day in his class, when he read Keats's 'The Eve of St. Agnes' aloud, I felt as if I were drunk on the marvelous words and images. A week later he asked me to stay after class."

"I can hear this one coming."

"Of course you can. But that's because you're ever so much cleverer than I was in those days. Anyway, he told me that I was the most talented student he'd ever had in any of his classes. I was so overwhelmed that I went back to my dorm room and cried."

"And when he asked you to begin helping him with his own work, you jumped at the chance to study at the master's feet."

"You sound as if you were there."

"It's not that unusual a story."

"Unfortunately, I suppose it's not. The day we got married, David's previous protégée phoned and offered her condolences. She went on to describe his penchant for seducing some naive, adoring coed every fall, only to drop her at the end of the year. If she'd only spoken up a little sooner . . ." Molly said wistfully.

"Would you have believed her?"

"Probably not. After all, I kept telling myself that he had married *me*. Surely, even if she were telling the truth, that proved he felt differently about me."

She lifted bare shoulders in a sad little shrug. "The mistake I made was in not realizing that rumors of his affairs had reached the administration, which frowned on professors becoming personally involved with students. Marrying me was David's way of setting up a very convenient smoke screen."

Taking a deep breath, she managed a crooked smile. "Oh, well, it just goes to show that everything works out for the best. If I hadn't taken that class, I probably wouldn't have stayed in school. And if I hadn't stayed in school, I wouldn't have seen your notice in that teacher's journal and if—"

He ducked his head and kissed her because once again it had been too long since the last time. "Are you trying to tell me that we have the jerk professor to thank for today?"

She chewed playfully on his lower lip. "I suppose, in a way, we do."

"Remind me to send the guy a thank-you card, then. When I'm not too busy."

Laughing delightedly, Molly rolled over so that she was lying full-length on him. "Okay. But I think you're going to be busy for a long, long time," she predicted as their mouths met.

This time she set the pace, and as he willingly followed her into the blinding mist, Cole realized that for the first time in his life he was entirely defenseless. And amazingly free.

THE RICH SCENT OF COFFEE woke her. Opening her eyes, Molly looked up to find Cole standing beside the bed, a mug in each hand.

"Morning," he greeted her cheerfully.

"Good morning." She pushed sleep-tumbled hair from her eyes as she sat up. "How long have you been up?"

"Awhile. I had some work to do."

"You should have wakened me."

He sat down on the edge of the bed. "Not much point in that. Unless you can ride fence or sort cattle."

Molly smiled her thanks as she accepted the coffee. "I'm afraid I'd be pretty useless," she admitted.

Cole's answering smile was slow and devastatingly attractive. "Oh, I wouldn't exactly say that," he murmured as he trailed a finger along her shoulder. "Can you ride?"

How was it that he could practically cause her to melt into the sheets with a mere touch? "Ride?"

He smoothed his finger tantalizingly down the slope of one of her breasts, inching under the dark sheet. "A horse. I thought I'd show you around the Double Diamond this morning. While we can do it by truck, it's a lot more fun on horseback."

Molly caught his hand. "I'd love a tour of the ranch, but if you don't stop that, Cole, I won't even be able to stand up, let alone stay on a horse."

"We could always stay here," he suggested hopefully.

"Uh-uh. It's been years since I've been riding. I can't think of a nicer way to spend a Sunday morning."

"Really? And here I thought you had such a vivid imagination."

"Speaking of imagination," she said softly, her eyes growing dark with sensual memories, "you're no slouch, cowboy."

He brushed his lips against hers. "It was good, wasn't it?"

"Better than good. And you sound surprised."

"Only at how terrific I feel this morning," he assured her. "By the way, all the hands love you."

"Oh?"

"I found two more breaks in the fence that were supposed to have been fixed last Thursday and was too mellow to yell at anyone."

"Mellow? Or worn out?"

He flashed her an appreciative grin. "Perhaps a little bit of both. Why don't you get dressed and I'll fix your breakfast."

"I don't eat breakfast," she answered automatically.

"You will this morning." He gave her a swift, hard kiss before leaving the room.

As she rose from the tangled sheets, reluctant to forsake their warmth and aroma that was a mixture of him, her and—the best part—the sweet redolence of their lovemaking, Molly told herself that his arrogant, high-handed attitude should have irritated her, but for some reason it didn't. By the time she had showered and dressed, she'd decided that Cole wasn't the only person who was unusually mellow this morning. Wasn't it funny what love could do?

Love? As the word reverberated in her mind, Molly froze. She was no better than so many of those teenagers she taught all day who confused sex with love. And that was precisely what she'd done. Wasn't it?

"Of course it is," she scolded herself as she walked down what seemed like miles of flagstones to the kitchen. "Face it, you've never experienced anything that begins to come close to yesterday. As long as you understand what you're dealing with, you can avoid getting hurt." *Lust*, she reiterated mentally. *That's all it is.* Defining it this way made her feel a great deal more sure of herself.

But as she entered the kitchen and was greeted by yet another of those breathtaking smiles, Molly's heart lurched and she was no longer sure of anything.

8

SOON THEY WERE RIDING across land still slick with dew. Against the horizon the cows, splendidly proportioned, their white faces contrasting handsomely with their dark red bodies, moved placidly. The cowboys sat erect in their saddles, and the horses were alert. The scene, a combination of easy rhythm and dynamic tension between the cattle and the mounted men, had a quality that Molly found almost lyrical.

When she admitted her feelings to Cole, he smiled understandingly. "It's tougher than it looks," he said. "Rounding up cattle is a lot like trying to move a bead of mercury with your fingers across a flat surface. You have to flow with the cattle. Although Herefords are generally easy to handle, any sudden movement spooks them. So you'd damned well better concentrate every single second. Let your mind wander once and they're gone."

"People say the Double Diamond is one of the most efficiently run ranches in the state," she offered. "They also say that's because you initiated a lot of changes your father refused to try."

"Times change."

"I suppose that's why I'm surprised to see the men working on horseback," she admitted.

"Pickups and planes are useful, but we still do most of our cattle work with horses. Horses are self-supporting, and on a ranch this large you're a long way ahead by using them."

"And of course it doesn't have anything to do with the fact that you'd rather be on a horse than in the cab of a pickup."

"Of course not," he lied with an easy grin.

As they continued to ride, Molly couldn't help making comparisons with her home state. She'd always loved the forested lands of West Virginia, where the mountains were so steep that the winter sun didn't begin to show over the gray-bearded peaks until nearly nine in the morning. The fall had always been her favorite season, when the hillsides glowed with asters, black-eyed Susans and goldenrod and autumn's bounty spread a country quilt of fiery color over the landscape. Only after leaving West Virginia had Molly fully appreciated the close relationship people there had to the land.

Chicago was admittedly an exciting city. A city of superlatives and extremes, always emphasizing its biggests, its bests, its firsts. After an initial bout of culture shock she'd come to enjoy all Chicago had to offer.

But the very things that had attracted Molly to the city were the same things she'd found unsettling. The city never rested; it was forever fixing up and tearing down. She hadn't even realized how much she was longing for the restfulness of the countryside until Cole's advertisement had caught her eye. Upon arriving in the county last September, Molly knew her spontaneous decision hadn't been a mistake. She'd felt instantly at home.

Not that eastern Oregon was anything like the forested hills of West Virginia. The vast land was bordered by hills of crumpled velvet. Shimmering fields of wheat and alfalfa rippled in the sunlit morning, and in a distant orchard the trees were wearing their spring colors of pink and white. The bright blue, cloudless sky seemed to go on forever.

"I understand why you did it," she said softly as they came to the top of a hill.

Cole reigned in his palomino quarter horse. "Did what?"

"Came home." Her eyes drank in the endless vista. "It's so magnificent. It's only right that you'd want to protect it."

He wasn't as surprised as he once might have been that Molly understood. "There's something about the land," he agreed, looking out over the acres of greening pastures. "I suppose part of the appeal is that God isn't making any more of it. Land is real, you can walk on it, see it, feel it, build a house on it." He shifted in the saddle in order to watch her expression. "Raise children on it."

She asked the question without thinking. "Do you want children, Cole?"

"You offering?"

It was back. The gritty tone, the distrust, the wall Cole could so expertly put up between himself and any woman who threatened to get too close. Molly had heard about Cole's ill-fated marriage and wondered if that were the cause. "She burned you badly, didn't she?"

Cole made a sound of sheer disgust as he pulled his hat lower over his eyes. "If you're talking about my former wife, you're way off base. You have to care before someone can hurt you."

"And you didn't care?"

"Not at the end. Want to take a break before starting back?"

They'd been riding all morning, and Molly, unaccustomed to spending long hours in the saddle, was sore. Her bottom had gone numb twenty minutes earlier, and her legs were growing stiff. "I thought you'd never ask," she said with a crooked smile as she dismounted.

"You ride better than I thought you would." He took her hand and led her to a spot under a poplar, where they sat in the grass.

His distant tone made her want to sigh. She smiled instead. "Oh, I'm just full of surprises. Remember?"

His cool black eyes displayed none of the fire of the night before. "I'm not likely to forget."

Pressing her knees against her chest, Molly wrapped her arms around them. "I'm not like her, you know."

He reached instinctively into his shirt pocket for a cigarette and found it empty. So he began shredding a piece of grass. "Like who?"

"Whoever hurt you."

"You can keep harping on it if you want, Molly. But I'll just keep telling you that you're wrong."

"Am I?" She rested her cheek on her knees as she studied him. "No, I don't think so. You don't trust me, Cole. And since I've never done anything to earn your mistrust, it's obvious that you feel that way about women in general."

"I didn't realize you'd earned a second degree in psychology."

"There are a lot of things you don't seem to realize." Frustrated by his brusque attitude, after all they'd shared, Molly jumped up and headed for her grazing mare.

He was beside her in an instant, grabbing the horse's bridle in one hand, Molly's arm in the other. "You've got one helluva short fuse, lady."

She glowered up at him. "You should know, since you keep lighting it. And for your information, Cole Murdock, most people find me quite agreeable. It's not my fault you keep confusing me with your ex-wife."

He laughed at that, but the sound had no mirth. "Sweetheart, there is no way I could ever confuse you with her. It'd be like mistaking fire for ice."

Her chin came up. "Which am I?"

Cole ran a placating hand slowly down her sleeve. His fingers closed over her hand, raising it slowly, deliberately to his lips. His gaze fixed on hers, he pressed a kiss against the tender skin of her palm. "What do you think?"

Lightning jolted through her veins. "I think you've got a lot of nerve, trying to seduce me when I'm furious with you."

"You're right." His teeth closed on the flesh at the base of her thumb. "I've got one helluva nerve."

"Dammit, Cole," she complained even as the caress thrilled her, "this is serious."

Cole studied her face and saw desire mingled with a very real distress. *Another rule broken,* he mused. "If I tell you about Laura, this one time, can we forget her?"

"I don't know," she answered quietly. "Can you?"

He swore. "You are, without a doubt, the most stubborn woman I've ever met."

"Thank you."

"It wasn't a compliment. See all those cattle?" he demanded suddenly.

Talk about ducking the issue, Molly thought as her eyes followed the broad sweep of his land. "I see them."

"Starting tomorrow, they're all going to have to be rounded up, sorted and branded. And as much as I'd love to spend the next week doing nothing but making mad, passionate love to you, I'm going to be working my tail off."

"Well, don't concern yourself with me," she countered. "I have my own work to do."

"I know. All the more reason for us not to be wasting the precious few hours we have."

As much as she hated to admit it, he had a point. "Her name was Laura?" she asked as she returned with him to sit in the shade. If she weren't already furious at the way the woman had taught Cole to mistrust, Molly would have hated her for her name alone. It sounded sleek. Elegant. Sophisticated. Everything she wasn't.

"That's right. Laura Westfall. Perhaps you've heard of her. Her father was—"

"Douglas Westfall, former secretary of the interior," Molly said flatly as her spirits sank even lower. Heard of her? Was there anyone in the western world who hadn't? Laura Westfall had sent the jet set soaring to new heights. The thought of her living here, on the Double Diamond, miles from Bergdorf Goodman, Cartier or "21" was amazing.

"I thought she was married to some Arabian prince."

"That was last year. This year it's a Grand Prix driver, although I'm not sure they bothered with the legalities."

"Oh."

Putting his arm around Molly, Cole drew her close. "I'd gone to Washington to testify before a government committee studying cutting back grazing permits. Douglas invited me to dinner, where I met his daughter."

"Lucky you."

"Lucky me," Cole drawled. "She'd just graduated from college and was at loose ends."

"So she married you because she was bored?"

He shrugged. "I think I represented a challenge. She saw me as a romanticized amalgam of John Wayne, Clint Eastwood and the Marlboro Man."

Despite the gravity of the subject, Molly smiled as she skimmed a finger along his jaw. "What a coincidence. That's the same way I see you."

He laughed. "You're good for me," he told her, sounding almost surprised. "Where the hell were you when I was twenty-one?"

Molly did some quick mental arithmetic. "Catching fireflies and ditching school to go fishing."

"I wish I'd known you then."

"You never would have noticed me," she said with a smile. "I wasn't the kind of girl boys wanted to look at."

"I would have looked."

"I was scrawny—all arms and legs."

"You were beautiful," he insisted. "I can imagine all the boys in West Virginia falling all over themselves to ask you out." He felt a surge of jealousy and controlled it.

"I've thought all along that you might be crazy, Cole Murdock," Molly said on a laugh. "Now I know you are."

His hand tunneled under her hair to curl around the back of her neck. "What would you say if I told you that I'm crazy about you? And have been since you first walked into my hotel room, looking like an angel who'd gotten lost on her way to paradise and ended up in Chicago."

Molly didn't think Cole would appreciate being laughed at, but she couldn't resist a smile. "I'd say that those are some pretty fanciful words for a cowboy."

"You inspire some pretty fanciful thoughts."

"You certainly took your own sweet time letting me know how you felt," she complained. "What if I had gone ahead and gotten involved with one of the other men around here? Like one of the Tomlin twins?"

"I would've gone after them with a shotgun," Cole answered without missing a beat.

Molly's eyes widened. "You're kidding."

His only answer was a careless shrug.

Molly pushed him back on the grass. "Tell me you're kidding," she demanded as she leaned over him.

Cole's smile was slow, wicked and decidedly devastating. "I'm kidding. Sort of," he tacked on as she exhaled a relieved breath. "Come here." He threaded his fingers through the golden strands of her hair and drew her lips down to his.

She was soft. So soft. And warm. Moist. And, oh, so very enticing. Cole moaned as he deepened the kiss, knowing that he was sinking slowly, inexorably into quicksand with each additional minute he spent with Molly.

When he finally lifted his head, his eyes were dark, swirling pools of need. "If we weren't here," he said, his fingers toying with the buttons of her shirt, "I'd undress you. Slowly."

She reached up and pressed her hand against his cheek. "Yes."

"Piece by piece, beginning with this red cotton shirt and ending up with that ridiculous scrap of lace between your legs."

"I thought you liked my underwear."

His eyes warmed in reminiscence. "I love every minuscule bit. I'm also pleased to discover that when you took my advice concerning practical clothing, you left something special for me to discover."

Molly lazily traced the planes and hollows of his rugged face with her fingertips. "What makes you think I bought it for you?"

He ran a hand possessively over her breasts. "Didn't you?"

"Of course I did. But it's bad strategy for me to admit it to you."

"I thought you didn't play games."

Molly sucked in a breath as his fingers spanned her midriff. Just the feel of his wide dark hand made her body grow warm and damp with wanting. "I have to do something," she argued. "We wouldn't want you outgrowing all your hats."

His hands moved to her back, slipping inside her waistband to press her more intimately against him. "That wouldn't be the only thing you're making me outgrow," he growled in her ear.

His voice was rough, but his eyes were tender as they looked into hers. Sunlight warmed her face. The robins had returned: she could hear them playing musical branches in the bright green leaves of the tree above them. A soft spring wind played in her hair. But as she stared into Cole's midnight-dark eyes, Molly was unaware of anything except the waves of love radiating through her.

"I think we can get arrested for the thoughts you're having," she said.

He laughed. "That's okay. The sheriff and I grew up together."

It was one of the few glimpses he'd given her of his past, and Molly savored it as she brushed back some black hair from his forehead. "Were you friends?"

"Sure. I gave him his first black eye."

"I wouldn't think that would endear you to him."

"Hell, he was responsible for my first broken leg."

"First?"

"I've broken a few bones. Back in my rodeo days," he admitted in a strange blend of cockiness and sheepishness that made Molly smile.

"Like this?" she asked, running a finger down his nose.

"Steer roping when I was thirteen. Damned thing kicked me."

"And this?" She massaged the knot on his collarbone she'd discovered during their lovemaking.

"Bronc."

"This?" She ran her hand down his side.

"That was from a bull named Satan back when I was too young and too stupid to know any better. He was, by the way, appropriately named."

"So it seems." A small line formed between her eyebrows. "Do you still ride bulls?"

He kissed her frowning lips. "No. And for the record, I didn't ride them then. If I'd managed to stay on, I probably wouldn't have provided such good target practice for Satan."

"I'm glad you don't do that anymore, Cole," Molly admitted solemnly. "I don't think I could stand it."

"Neither could I. That's why I stopped."

"How was the sheriff responsible for you breaking your leg? The first time."

"Well, he was a long way from being the sheriff back then. We were both about eleven, and his dad had just bought this gorgeous black Arabian stallion. We knew he hadn't been broken yet, but that made him even more appealing to a couple of kids. When Jimmy dared me to ride him, I couldn't resist."

"Sounds as if you couldn't ride him, either," Molly pointed out. "You must've driven your mother crazy."

His eyes turned to black ice, his voice chilled. "Not really."

Molly's own experience taught her that no matter how old one became, one could never quite stop being someone's child. "It was her, wasn't it?" she asked softly. "The one who first taught you not to trust."

"That," he said slowly, firmly, "is one of the most ridiculous things I've ever heard."

They stared at each other for a long, drawn-out moment, faces close together. Cole's expression was remote and cold, Molly's openly empathic.

"All right," she said finally. "I can read a No Trespassing sign when I see one, Cole. I won't push."

"Good." He looked up at the sky. Overhead an eagle was flying in lazy circles. Usually the sight gave him pleasure. Not today. Not now. "We'd better be getting back."

Molly rose reluctantly from the fragrant meadow grass. "Have you gotten any better at breaking horses?" she asked conversationally as they returned to the ranch. Cole had remained uncomfortably silent.

He shrugged. "I like to think so. I break all the horses on the Double Diamond."

"It must be difficult."

Cole knew what she was doing, and a part of him appreciated it. Another distant part of him searched for false sympathy in her tone. When he didn't find it, he relaxed slightly.

"You need patience. And a gentle hand. There are a lot of sorry horses in the world, and most of them have been made sorry by the men who broke them." He patted the palomino's neck absently. "We had a foreman when I was growing up who was a mean-tempered old son of a bitch. Dad must've fired him a hundred times, but he always took him back."

"Why?"

"Because he knew cattle," Cole answered simply. "Anyway, I was about seven when old Garth bought a sweet little mare from Dad. I'd wanted her for my own, so I'd go out and watch him work with her every day." He shook his head at the memory. "Before he was through, Garth had managed to impose all his own flaws on that horse, and when he was forced to live with those flaws every day, he began to curse the horse. He finally had to get rid of her."

"That's terrible."

"Common sense tells you that what you put into a horse, you'll get out of her. Treat a horse with patience, and you'll get a horse that'll give you everything she's got. There's a knack to breaking in a good horse," he said, giving her that slow, wicked smile she hadn't been certain she'd ever see again. "Kind of like there's a knack for—"

Molly held up her hand in warning. "If you dare say it, Cole Murdock, I'll show you exactly how the Hatfields got their reputation for orneriness."

Before she realized his intention, Cole had reached over, cupped her chin in his fingers and planted a hard, wet kiss against her lips. "I love it when you talk dirty, lady."

Laughter bubbled up from lips that refused to obey her command not to smile. "Dammit, Cole, one of these days you're going to take me seriously."

His eyes, shaded by the brim of the black Stetson, turned too dark to read. "Now that's where you're wrong," he drawled. "I take you real seriously, Molly. I always have."

Molly was trying to decide exactly how to comment on that when a plane flew overhead, glistening silver in the afternoon sun. Spooked by the faint roar, a group of yearlings suddenly bolted from a nearby herd, each animal following the one in front of him. Acting instinctively, Cole swung out, hunched over the palomino. Arrowheads of earth flew from the horse's hooves.

Molly caught her breath when he suddenly swerved in front of the cattle, joined by two other hands who began working the runaways that had veered out behind Cole. Within minutes the restless cattle had rejoined the herd.

"That was wonderful," she exclaimed when he returned. "I'm very impressed."

Cole's gaze drifted over the flowing fields dotted with the red-and-white cattle. "My father taught me two important things," he murmured, "the first being that you can't send a man to do anything unless you're willing to do it yourself. And you can't make a man work harder than you're willing to work. It's just that simple."

"For something so simple, there are an awful lot of people in this world who haven't caught on."

"That's because they didn't have Garrett Murdock for a father."

"It probably wasn't easy being his son."

Cole shrugged. "I wouldn't know. I do remember one time, when I was little, he sent me out after a cow that had wandered off. I couldn't find that damned cow for the life of me, and about dinnertime I decided I'd looked as long as anybody would. I'd no sooner ridden into the yard when Dad came roaring out, jerked me off the saddle in front of the hands and really dressed me down. Point was, of course, to make me cry in front of the men."

"Did you?" Molly asked, guessing the answer ahead of time.

"No. After a while he put me back on the saddle and told me that if I wasn't man enough to cut it on the Double Diamond, then I might as well not come home."

"What happened then?"

"I found the cow." It was a simple answer but laced with the steel Molly had come to expect.

"Is that how you plan to treat your children?" she asked quietly. Personally, she was distressed by the story but knew better than to state her feelings.

He gave her a long, steady look. "I've already told you that there are a lot of different ways to handle horses and people, Molly. Garrett Murdock's way isn't my way. And it never was."

They'd reached the paddock. Although Molly was more than capable of dismounting herself, she didn't argue when Cole gripped her around the waist and lifted her down. She found herself welcoming any excuse to feel those strong hands anywhere on her body.

"I'd like to take you home—"

"But you have work to do," she finished for him. "I've already kept you too long. Besides, I've got my own car, remember?"

Cole's eyes, as they seemed to search hers for hidden meanings, displayed lingering doubt. He'd never met a city woman who understood that ranching was a seven-day-a-week job. "Sure you don't mind?"

She rose onto her toes and pressed her lips against his. "Positive. Have a good roundup."

It didn't take long to retrieve her things from the house. As he walked her out to her car and opened the door for her to get in, Cole was noticeably quiet. Molly wondered whether he'd simply run out of things to say to her, or if he could possibly be thinking he'd miss her. As she already knew she would miss him.

"There's a Cattlemen's Association dance this Saturday night," he said, leaning a hand on the roof of her car as he bent to give her a kiss.

"I know." Molly forced her hands to remain steady as she put the key in the ignition. "I've been looking forward to it."

"You're going with me."

She glanced up at him. Amusement danced in her eyes. "Why, Cole Murdock," she drawled, "are you by any chance asking me for a date?"

"You're going to make this tough on me, aren't you?" he asked, grimacing as he heard his own words tossed back at him.

Molly nodded. "Absolutely."

Cole hitched his fingers uncomfortably in his belt loops. "I suppose I am."

She grinned. "About time, too, cowboy."

Cole remained where he was for a long, thoughtful time, watching as Molly drove away in a cloud of dust. A very large part of him was strongly tempted to get back on his horse, chase her down and ask her to stay.

"You've got work to do," he muttered under his breath as he turned back toward the paddock. "And you damn well can't do it properly mooning after the woman like a lovesick bull."

But as he rejoined the men in the far pasture, Cole discovered that putting Molly Fairchild out of his mind was easier said than done.

9

MOLLY RETURNED HOME to find Barbara at work in the kitchen. Chicken soup bubbling on the stove made her mouth water.

"That smells out of this world," she said with a smile. "But you certainly didn't need to go to this much trouble. After all, you must have just gotten home."

"We got home last night."

"Last night?" she asked absently as she lifted the pot lid and inhaled deeply. "Wasn't the skiing any good?"

"I wouldn't know." Barbara reached into a drawer and pulled out a peach place mat and matching linen napkin.

Molly replaced the lid and turned back to Barbara, her green eyes filled with regret. "Oh, no. I knew I should have gone along to run interference. You and Mike had a fight, didn't you? That's why you're back so soon."

"We didn't fight," Barbara said calmly, taking a tray from a lower cupboard.

"Then what happened?"

"Mike broke his leg. On the first run."

Molly whitened. "Where is he? Upstairs?"

Barbara's red curls bounced on her shoulders as she shook her head. "Of course not. The poor man certainly couldn't make it up all those steep stairs, Molly. Not in a cast."

Poor man? This from Barbara? "I wasn't thinking," Molly apologized. "So where is he?"

"I moved him into the den. With the television, the VCR, stereo, his beloved Gertie and some computer magazines I stole from the hospital's emergency waiting room. They're old, but he says he's never read them." She flashed Molly a brilliant smile as she placed a crystal bud vase on the tray. "Isn't that lucky?"

Molly stared at the perky daisy Barbara was putting in the vase. "Lucky." She doubted that there was a computer magazine anywhere in the world that Mike Baker had not read. "Well, I suppose I ought to check on him."

"Tell him I'll bring his supper in to him in just a minute."

Barbara waiting on the Sultan of Software? That was a switch. Molly was tempted to run upstairs and get her camera so that she could preserve the scene for posterity.

"Looks like you're out of the Olympics," she said as she entered the den.

Someone—it had to have been Barbara—had made him a bed on the couch, complete with fluffy pillows and a hand-quilted comforter Molly recognized as one Barbara had worked on for months. An empty beer bottle rested on the coffee table, magazines were scattered over the floor and a bright needlepoint pillow emblazoned with tropical birds propped up the white plaster cast on Mike's leg.

He grinned sheepishly. "That's what I get for show-ing off."

"Aha, so there was a bunny on the mountain."

The last time the three of them had taken a ski trip, during the Christmas vacation, Mike's moves in the lodge had been every bit as smooth and practiced as those on the slopes. The trip, Molly remembered, had turned out to be a disaster, with Mike seeming deter-mined to win the gold medal for indoor sports and Barbara growing more and more out of sorts with each passing day.

"Hey," Mike complained, "you just happen to be talking about the woman I love."

Love? "Fast work," Molly said. "Does this brave woman happen to have a name?"

"Here you are, darling," Barbara trilled as she swept into the room, tray in hand. "I hope you like it."

"How could I not?" Mike countered, his expression warming intimately. "Since I'm wild about the cook."

Molly stared, mouth agape, as Barbara giggled like a schoolgirl. "You romantic devil." She lowered herself gracefully to the edge of the couch and ran her fingers playfully through his hair.

Mike was smiling as he kissed her. "Just wait until I get rid of this cast. Then we'll give romance an entirely new meaning," he promised huskily.

Molly cleared her throat. "Excuse me, but what were you two drinking up on the mountain?"

"Drinking?" Barbara asked vaguely as she lovingly tucked the linen napkin into the top of Mike's green-

and-red plaid pajamas. "We didn't have anything to drink, did we, darling?"

"Not a drop, sweetheart. I don't need artificial stimulants when I'm around you."

"Isn't he wonderful?" Barbara asked, smiling beatifically up at Molly.

"Wonderful," she agreed dryly. "Is it my imagination, or have I missed a chapter somewhere along the way?"

"You haven't missed anything," Mike assured her. "Except one terrific weekend."

"How terrific could it be? In case you've forgotten, you happen to have broken your leg."

"Luckiest break of my life," he agreed cheerfully.

Molly shook her head. "I've always known you were crazy, Mike Baker, but this takes the cake."

"Mike's telling the truth," Barbara said as she adoringly watched him sip the robust chicken broth. "When I saw him tumbling down the side of that mountain, totally out of control, I thought for sure he was going to die."

"And that's when she finally realized that she loved me," Mike explained. "Mmm, delicious as usual, cupcake."

"Are you sure? I didn't put in too much thyme?"

"The thyme's perfect."

"Salt. Is it too salty?"

Mike pressed his fingers to his lips. "Ambrosia."

"You don't have to lie to me. I want things to be perfect for my brave, strong man."

Molly had had about enough. "It's perfect. It's always perfect. Everything you do is perfect. At least it has been up until now. Because you two are disgusting."

"Just wait until *you* fall in love, Molly," Barbara said serenely, "and we'll see what you think then."

"What makes you think I haven't?"

Barbara slowly lowered the spoon to the bowl as both she and Mike stared up at Molly. "I knew it. You're in love with Cole Murdock."

"No. Maybe. I don't know, but I think I might be. A little." She hadn't planned to tell anyone about those unruly feelings, but faced with Mike and Barbara's besotted state, Molly had been unable to resist.

"That's so wonderful!" Barbara was on her feet, hugging Molly.

"Congratulations, Molly," Mike said with the enthusiasm of a man who's discovered his own pleasure in love. "It couldn't have happened to a nicer lady. Except, of course, Babs. Not that you're not super, too, but it's just that—"

"I understand," Molly broke in. "Perfectly."

"We'll have to have Cole over for a celebration dinner," Barbara reflected. "Rack of lamb would be nice, don't you think? Or perhaps, since he's a rancher, we ought to stick to prime rib."

"We're not having a celebration dinner," Molly insisted. She was beginning to wish she hadn't brought the subject up.

Mike arched a puzzled brow. "Why not?"

"Because Cole doesn't know how I feel."

"Oh, dear," Barbara said softly, "you're not letting that silly rumor about Cole and Marlene Young stand in your way, are you?"

"What rumor?"

Barbara and Mike exchanged a guilty look. "The one going around about them getting married," Mike mumbled.

Molly prided herself on not flinching. "Cole isn't going to marry Marlene." As soon as she'd spoken the words, Molly realized that she, for one, believed them.

"Of course he's not," Barbara agreed loyally. "So what's the problem?"

"The problem is that Cole isn't going to marry anyone. Including me. Because he's definitely not in love."

There was a sudden silence in the room. Molly felt as if she were under a powerful microscope as two pairs of eyes studied her intently.

"Of course he is," Barbara insisted.

"You bet," Mike chimed in. "He just doesn't know it yet."

"He's like me." Barbara's meticulously manicured fingernails gleamed like rubies as she placed her hand lovingly, possessively, on Mike's arm. "Don't worry, Molly, give the man time. He'll catch on."

"And if he doesn't, we'll just have to help him see the light," Mike volunteered.

Molly glared at them warningly. "If either one of you dares to say a single word to him, so help me, I'll . . . I'll . . . I don't know what I'll do," she admitted. "But it won't be pretty."

"Goodness, Molly, how you do carry on." Barbara serenely resumed feeding her newly discovered love. "But don't worry, we promise not to interfere." She smiled confidently. "The way Cole's been looking at you, it won't be necessary."

Wishing she could feel as confident about her chances, Molly retreated to the kitchen where she helped herself to some chicken soup. As happy as she was for Barbara and Mike, Molly couldn't help feeling a tinge of envy.

THE CALL CAME A LITTLE after 2:00 a.m., shattering the night. Fumbling in the dark, Molly managed to pick the receiver up on the third ring.

"Hello?" She was instantly awake. The last time the telephone had rung in the middle of the night, it had been the hospital, alerting her that Loretta had disappeared again. When the operator asked Molly if she'd accept the long-distance charges, her fear turned to annoyance.

"Molly, I'm so glad I caught you home!"

"Do you know what time it is here in Oregon, Loretta?" Molly glanced over at the clock radio on the bedside table. "I'm usually at home at two-fifteen in the morning. Just in case the phone happens to ring. You never know who might call. What's the problem?"

"Problem? Why, there's no problem. What makes you think that?"

Experience, Molly could have answered. "Sorry," she said instead, forcing herself to remain patient. "What's up?"

"I have the most exciting news." Even over the long-distance phone line Molly could tell that her mother was floating on air. "I'm going to record an album."

Molly leaned back against the pillow and dragged her hands through her hair. *Here we go again,* she thought wearily. "I know. With Jerry Lee Lewis, right?"

There was a pause on the other end of the line. "Where on earth would you get an idea like that, Molly?" Loretta asked finally. "I don't even know Jerry Lee Lewis. Not that I wouldn't love to meet him. Anyway, I met this wonderful man. His name is Marty, and he's a big record producer in Nashville. He heard me sing at this evening's talent show and said that he's never heard a voice as sweet and pure as mine. So he's insisting on a recording session. It's going to be a solo album. It's the one, Molly. I can just feel it in my bones."

"The one?"

"That's goin' make me a star, sweetie pie. Just you wait. By this time next year, Loretta Belle's goin' be queen of the Grand Ole Opry."

Frustration mingled with regret for lost opportunities caused Molly to close her eyes for a long, thoughtful moment.

"Molly? You still there?"

"I'm still here. Congratulations."

"I'll send you a free copy, as soon as it's released," Loretta promised.

"I'll be looking forward to it," Molly murmured, knowing that by this time the next day Loretta would have forgotten all about her fictional producer and his alleged recording session.

"You and me both, baby." Loretta was laughing as she hung up.

Try as she might, Molly couldn't get back to sleep. She told herself that she should be grateful that Loretta's manic-depressive personality was on an upswing. The problem was, it was during such times that her mother's behavior became most bizarre. Molly felt so far away. So helpless. If only she could bring Loretta out to Oregon, where she could keep an eye on her, then she'd feel a great deal better.

But then, as she thought back over the time she'd spent with Cole, Molly was forced to admit that their fledgling relationship was shaky enough without bringing her mother into it. Her deep-seated sense of obligation warred with her desire for a life of her own. A love of her own. By the time the sun had risen, Molly still didn't have an answer to what was threatening to be a very difficult decision.

"I CAN'T BELIEVE YOU TWO talked me into this," Molly complained four days later.

Looking around Mike's classroom, she had the strange feeling that she'd suddenly stumbled into a mad scientist's laboratory. Which wasn't that far off mark, she decided, watching Mike examine a device purported to scramble an egg while it was still inside the shell.

"Isn't this great?" He held the invention up. "Think of it. Thanks to this little gizmo, some day the astronauts could be eating scrambled eggs on the moon."

"They've already been to the moon, and they had artificial orange juice," Molly pointed out. "Tell me one more time what I'm doing here."

"You're helping judge Mike's young inventors' competition," Barbara said from across the room. "This is nice," she added. "An electric ice-cream scoop. I think we should try it. I'll go get some ice cream from the home ec lab." She left the room.

"You're actually going to plug that thing in?" Molly asked dubiously.

"Kyle's one of my best students," Mike assured her. "I'm sure it'll be safe."

Barbara returned with a quart of double dutch, which she placed on the table. Molly backed up as Mike turned on the invention. She was relieved when there were no sparks.

"It says you have to wait ninety seconds for it to heat up," he read from the proposal.

"Wouldn't it be exciting if one of the kids actually invented something that made millions and millions of dollars?" Barbara said enthusiastically.

"I'll be happy if we can just get through this without one of the kids burning the school down," Molly muttered.

Mike touched his finger experimentally to the stainless steel scoop. "Spoilsport. I thought you were so hot on getting kids to use their talents."

"I've never seen a poem or short story capable of spontaneous combustion," Molly countered.

"I think it's ready," Barbara interrupted.

"Here we go, ready or not." Mike pressed the scoop onto the block of ice cream.

Molly watched the chocolate begin melting and spreading across the table to drip onto the floor. "So much for millions and millions of dollars."

"Hey, all he needs to do is slightly adjust his temperature control," Mike argued. "Here, Molly, try these slippers on." He held out what looked to be a pair of fluorescent pink rabbits who'd seen better days.

"Thanks, anyway, but I think I'll leave that honor to you."

"They don't fit me. Come on, Molly, be a sport."

"I'm already spending my one free afternoon judging the Young Inventors' Gong Show," she countered. "You don't call that being a good sport?"

"You've been an angel," he agreed placatingly. "But this is the final entry, and if you don't put them on, we'll never know if they work. They're supposed to be weight sensitive."

Molly sighed as she kicked off her running shoes and tugged on the bright pink slippers. "Now what?" She held up her hand. "I know. I click my heels together three times and end up in Kansas."

"Very funny. They're flashlight slippers. So you don't have to fumble for a light switch in the dark," he explained. "Walk across the room."

Molly took a few steps. The bright lights sewn into the toes of the fuzzy slippers flashed each time her foot touched the floor. "They're terrific if you're looking for a job as a walking strobe light."

"They need a bit more work," Mike agreed. "I vote for the electric bathroom mirror defogger."

"I like the battery-operated sifter" was Barbara's vote.

"The one that exploded flour all over the room?" Molly asked.

Barbara shrugged. "You used the wrong speed."

"This is ridiculous," Molly said with an exasperated sigh. "None of this stuff works. How're we supposed to judge a winner?"

Barbara's gaze moved toward the open doorway. "Speaking of winners," she murmured. "Why, Cole Murdock, what a nice surprise. You're just in time to cast the deciding ballot."

Cole grinned as he glanced down at Molly's fuzzy pink feet. "If we're voting for most original dress by a teacher, Molly gets my vote, hands down."

Molly wished the ground would open up and swallow her whole—ridiculous slippers and all. "There's an explanation for this."

He tipped his hat back with his thumb. "There always is," he agreed mildly. "That's one of the things I admire about you, Molly. You definitely throw yourself into your work." His laughing eyes darkened with unmistakable desire as his gaze left her feet and settled on her face.

"Well, my goodness, will you look at the time," Barbara said brightly. "I had no idea it had gotten so late. Come along, Michael, I have a roast at home waiting to go into the oven."

"But what about . . . Right," Mike said, belatedly getting the point. "Can't keep that old rib roast waiting. Nice to see you again, Cole."

"I've just had a marvelous idea," Barbara said. "How would you like to drop by for dinner, Cole?" Molly doubted that many men could resist Barbara's warm, encouraging smile. "We'd love to have you, wouldn't we, Molly?"

"I'm sure Cole's too busy with branding to socialize," Molly replied evenly, biting back her frustration at her friend's heavy-handed matchmaking.

"I'm sorry, Barbara," Cole apologized. "But I do have to get back to the ranch. I only drove into town because there was something I had to discuss with Molly."

"Well, don't let us stop you," Barbara trilled. "Come on, Michael. That big old piece of beef won't roast itself." As he fumbled with his crutches, she practically dragged him from the room.

"I'm sorry about that," Molly said when they were alone.

He shrugged. "They're your friends. It's only natural they'd want to meddle a little the first time you began seeing someone."

Was that what they were doing? Seeing each another? Molly could think of several more accurate descriptions but kept them to herself. "Now here's something you might be interested in," she said brightly, suddenly desperate to change the subject. "Lori Matthews invented it, and although it still needs to have a few bugs worked out, Mike thinks it has great potential."

Cole took the heavy iron bar from her hand. "A branding iron?"

"A portable one. For out on the range."

He turned it over, studying it curiously. "Where's the battery pack?"

Molly's laughter bubbled free. "That's the only problem. It weighs seventy-five pounds, so Lori couldn't lift it."

He smiled. "Looks as if Lori better stick to playing the piano."

"That's what I told Mike," Molly agreed. "What did you want to talk about?"

"First things first. Come here."

The bright yellow lights on Molly's slippers flashed on and off as she closed the gap between them, but neither she nor Cole noticed. "How's that?" she asked softly, standing so that their bodies were barely touching.

"Not quite close enough." He brushed his knuckles down her cheek. "You've got flour on your face again."

"One of the hazards of invention judging," she said as she went up on her toes.

As their mouths touched, Cole's breath shuddered out and his hands tightened around her waist. From the gleam in his eyes Molly had expected his lips to be hard, demanding, to plunder her mouth as they had on so many exciting occasions. But instead, Cole seemed determined to take his time, to keep the pace restrained, his lips gentle. Tender. And so wonderfully, remarkably sweet. A slow warmth began to build inside her.

Sweet. She was so unbelievably sweet. As Cole allowed himself to drift on waves of warm pleasure, it crossed his mind that he couldn't remember ever feeling so relaxed with a woman. Even one he wanted as much as he did Molly. The feeling of contentment was as unexpected as it was satisfying, and as he kissed her leisurely, lingeringly, Cole decided not to try to unravel the mystery now. There would be plenty of time for that later. Back at the Double Diamond. Right now he only wanted to revel in the taste of her sensually soft lips, the feel of her slender body pressing against his.

"I needed that," he murmured into her hair when the slow, infinitely tender kiss finally came to an end.

"Me, too."

He tilted his head back and looked down into her smiling face. "Do you have any idea how much I've missed you these past four days?"

Molly found the admission overwhelmingly thrilling. "Yes."

"I would've come sooner, but—"

She pressed her hand against his cheek. He smelled faintly of leather and sandalwood. She found it a potent combination. "You had to work."

"I know it's hard for someone who hasn't grown up on a ranch to understand that we don't punch time clocks."

She wondered if Laura Westfall had been one of those who hadn't understood, and guessed that probably she had. If all those gossip columns were even vaguely accurate, one of the things Cole's former wife excelled at was the continuous pursuit of pleasure. How willing would she have been to sit idly by, waiting for Cole to come in from the range? Not very, Molly answered herself.

"I'm well acquainted with hard work, Cole," Molly said seriously.

He studied her. "I suppose you are.... There's something I need to ask you."

Her pulse skipped a beat. "Oh?"

As he suddenly released her, then jammed his hands deep into his back pockets, Molly could tell that he was uncomfortable with his planned topic, and she felt some misgivings.

His hand left his pocket long enough to pick up one of the inventions on a nearby table. It resembled a two-inch television in a self-sealing plastic bag, but Molly had the feeling he wasn't really looking at it at all. "I've been thinking about last weekend."

"So have I.... I think this is where I tell you I had a wonderful time."

"Me, too." His expression made him look like a man on the way to the gallows.

"But?" Molly prompted, preparing herself for the little speech about how he hoped that she hadn't misunderstood his intentions. That while the sex was great, he really wasn't in the market for a relationship right now. She was a nice woman, but ... etc., etc., etc.

"I realized I took something for granted," he mumbled.

"I see," she answered calmly, not seeing anything at all.

Cole turned around, pinning her with an unnervingly direct gaze. "I assumed that you were protected," he said. "After all, you're certainly beyond the age of consent, and women these days usually take care of such things. Besides, I gave you plenty of advance warning about how I felt about you, and how I wanted you, and you appeared to return those feelings and . . . Oh, hell." His voice dropped off as he stared at her. "Well?"

Her temper flared at the way he'd so cavalierly lumped her together with all his other women. "Well?" she asked, vaguely, as if she still hadn't gotten the drift. Oh, she'd tell him the truth, Molly decided. But first she had every intention of making him work for it.

"Did you use something? The pill, an IUD?"

Molly wondered who he thought he was, disregarding the possibility of pregnancy for two long days of lovemaking, then showing up here behaving as if he actually suspected her of somehow planning to trap him.

"You needn't worry, Cole," she said coolly. "If anything happens, I certainly won't bother you."

Cole dropped the combination underwater television and alarm clock to the floor. "If anything happens," he growled, grabbing her by the arms, "you can be damned certain I'll see to it that you and the child— my child—are well taken care of."

His eyes burned with a murderous dark fury that astounded her. Molly lifted her chin. "You have no idea how that relieves my mind," she said, keeping her eyes level and her voice calm. "But if you were a real gentleman, Cole, you'd take your hands off me. You're going to leave bruises."

He'd never been rough with a woman before. Not even Laura, who, God knows, had certainly tempted him. There had only been that one time he'd almost lost his self-control—the day she'd taunted him with the abortion he'd known nothing about until it had been too late. It had taken a Herculean effort, but he'd managed to control his temper until he left the room. Cole flexed his fingers as he remembered the broken hand he'd gotten from slamming his left fist into the brick wall of the kitchen.

"If you are pregnant," he said in a low, rough tone that Molly found a great deal more threatening than the harshest shout, "I have a right to know."

Although she knew that the argument was escalating out of control, Molly found his arrogant attitude infuriating. "Even if I were pregnant, what makes you think the baby would be yours? You're certainly not the only man in the county, Cole Murdock."

"Because you told me that there's been no one else but that damned professor." He spoke with a quiet deliberation as he struggled to hold his temper in check.

She tossed her head. "And you believed that? From a woman capable of cold-bloodedly planning a pregnancy?"

His eyes kindled at that and Cole remembered how only minutes ago he'd felt unexpectedly tender toward Molly. Right now, however, he was blindly furious. He was unaccustomed to such wild mood swings; no one had ever been able to destroy his iron control this way.

No one until Molly, Cole corrected grimly, wondering if there would ever be any middle ground where this woman was concerned.

"Even if I hadn't believed you," he returned evenly, in that soft, dangerous voice, "your body's incapable of lying."

"Cole." She pressed a trembling hand against his chest, momentarily sidetracked by the wild, out-of-control heartbeat she felt beneath her fingertips. "I should have told you."

Strong fingers, which had loosened slightly at her complaint, now dug more deeply into her skin. "Told me what?"

"That I'm on the pill. And have been for the past three months."

"Three months?"

As she watched the distrust flash into his black eyes, Molly wondered dejectedly if he would ever be able to accept her at face value. "I've always had erratic periods; this past year they've gotten worse, so the doctor prescribed the pills in order to regulate my cycle. So now that we have that all settled, are there any more little items you'd like cleared up before you ride on back to the safety of the Double Diamond?"

Cole didn't like her implication. She made him feel uncharacteristically defensive. "You make it sound as if I'm hiding out there."

"Aren't you?" Molly challenged quietly. She gave him a long, searching look. "I really do feel sorry for you, Cole. Whenever you begin to open up, to allow yourself to feel some honest emotions, you start posting all those damned No Trespassing signs."

His face was a granite mask. "When I want to be psychoanalyzed, Ms Fairchild, I'll ask."

"Fine. And when I want to be treated like a cheap, one-night stand, Mr. Murdock, I'll know where to go."

It was the pain in her eyes contrasting with the ice in her voice that proved to be Cole's downfall. He muttered a self-deprecating oath as he lowered his forehead to hers. "I've been a jackass, haven't I?"

Molly could feel the fury flowing out of her, replaced by something that more than ever resembled love. "Yes, you have."

Cole sighed heavily. "How do you know me so well, Molly Fairchild?" he asked quietly. He was speaking as much to himself as to her.

Molly swallowed. "I know pain," she said softly. "And rejection... There are admittedly a great many distinctions between my past life in West Virginia and yours here in Oregon. But some things don't come with regional differences, Cole. They hurt wherever you are."

Once again Cole felt something move through him, stronger and more insistent than any emotion he'd ever known. Once again he couldn't quite put his finger on precisely what it was. "I'm beginning to think I don't deserve you," he said finally, looking down at her with grave, guarded eyes.

"Funny you should mention that since I'm beginning to think the same thing," she agreed with a faint smile. When she saw that his dark eyes had become shuttered once again, Molly took pity on him. "But for now, it looks like you're stuck with me."

"For now," he agreed, wondering why that idea no longer satisfied him. Then he lowered his head, and as his lips touched hers, Cole forgot to think.

10

IF MOLLY HAD BEEN WORRIED about how eagerly she had been awaiting Saturday night, she knew she was sunk when she opened the door and found Cole standing on the front porch. He was dressed in a charcoal-gray suit that would have looked at home on Wall Street were it not for its vaguely Western cut. He'd foregone the usual black Stetson, but as Molly glanced down at his feet, she smiled to see the sleek gray eelskin boots.

After greeting her with a kiss, Cole wolf-whistled softly as he drank in the sight of Molly, dressed in an off-the-shoulder peasant-style dress. The embroidered hem of her wide skirt ended in scallops at midcalf.

"I've got an idea," he said.

The obvious hunger in his dark eyes thrilled her. "What's that?"

"Instead of going to the dance, why don't I throw you over my shoulder, take you into the house, toss you on the nearest sofa and make love to you until neither of us can move?"

"Sorry. Mike's got possession of the nearest sofa."

"Damn. If he wasn't such an extraordinary teacher, I'd fire him on the spot for single-handedly destroying my love life." Cole trailed a caressing hand down her smiling face. "Later."

Molly was unprepared for the way the softly spoken promise caused her pulse to quicken. "Later," she agreed in a whisper.

"What happened to the Blazer?" she asked as he led her to a sleek black Ferrari parked at the curb.

"I thought we'd established that this is a date," he replied as he opened the passenger door for her. "I figured this would be more appropriate under the circumstances."

"It reminds me of Darth Vader's personal warship," Molly said as Cole joined her in the car's cockpit-like interior.

"That bad, huh?"

She ran her fingers over the glove-soft leather seat. "I think this is another one of those trick questions. If I tell you I love your car, you'll accuse me of being one of those materialistic women who's only interested in a man's bankbook, but if I lie and—"

He lifted his hand and gently cupped the back of her neck. "Molly, it's not a trick question. You're allowed to like the car for itself. In fact, if you want to know the truth, I get a kick out of it every time I get behind the wheel."

"I can imagine." She surveyed the dashboard, which looked as if it had come from the *Star Trek* prop department. "It must be absolutely exhilarating."

Cole tilted his head, and for a moment Molly thought he was going to kiss her. But instead, he merely studied her thoughtfully.

"Get out," he said suddenly.

"Out?"

"Unless you want to climb over the gearshift, which would probably be a bit difficult in that skirt and those high heels."

"Why would I want to do that?"

His dark eyes, illuminated by the silver light of a full moon, brimmed with patient affection. "Because it's a little difficult to drive from the passenger seat."

Her heart trebled its beat. "You're kidding."

"Nope."

"You're going to let me drive your car? This car?"

"Sure." He'd begun to open his door before turning back toward her. "You do know how to work a floor shift, don't you?"

"Of course I do." She wrapped her arms around him. "You're a sweet, wonderful man, Cole. Even if you do try to hide it!"

The fire was instantaneous, exploding in a blazing ball of heat and flame. Molly's lips parted with what could have been a moan but sounded more like a sob, inviting the bold thrust of his tongue. Her desperate hands delved beneath his jacket to move frantically up and down his back. She trembled deliciously when his hands slipped inside the neckline of her dress to caress her breasts. When she touched him, her palm pressing against his stiffness, Cole thought he'd explode.

His fevered mind quickly considered the possibilities. He could take her here, now, as his body was aching to do. It had been six long days since he'd felt her firm, womanly flesh next to his. Six even longer nights since he'd felt those slim legs wrapped around his waist. His body was ready—more than ready. As, it appeared, was hers. He promptly discarded the idea. Although it might actually be possible to make love in a Ferrari, Cole wanted something a great deal more than a brief, fumbling, frantic coupling.

He could return tō the house, throw Mike off the sofa and take her there, her body gleaming in the firelight as it had a week ago. Or he could carry her upstairs to her room. Cole liked the idea of making love to Molly in her bed, leaving sensual memories that would linger once he'd returned to the ranch.

The ranch. They could go there. The only problem was that the Double Diamond was thirty-five miles away. If they kept this up, they'd wreck the car before covering the first five miles.

"This isn't going to work," he said finally as he broke the kiss.

Molly's head was spinning. She could only stare up at him.

"You living here." He jerked his dark head in the direction of the house. "Me out at the Double Diamond. I want you to move in with me."

"Cole, I can't," she protested softly.

"The hell you can't," he argued in a tone that she had no doubt was effective on both ranch hands and cattle alike. "I've ached for you, Molly. I thought that after we'd made love, that ache would lessen. Even go away."

"And?"

"It hasn't. It's worse than ever."

Although Cole's expression was about as grim as Molly had ever seen it, she couldn't deny that his words thrilled her. Unwilling to let him see the pleasure in her eyes, she dropped her gaze to her lap.

With a soft curse Cole caught her jaw in his hand, lifting her face to his. "I'm not used to feeling this way. And I damn well don't like it."

"Do you think I do?" she asked quietly.

His dark eyes swept her face. Moonlight filtered through the branches of a nearby tree, touching her emerald eyes with silvery lights. "I don't know what to think."

Molly decided to play it light. For now. "Why don't you give the matter some thought while I drive to the Grange?" She held out her hand for the keys.

Her lightness didn't solve his problem. But it did smooth over the moment, Cole decided. "When I drove up here tonight, I was considering skipping the dance entirely," he admitted. "I've never really enjoyed these things. But now that I see you, I've decided I rather like the idea of showing you off."

She shook her head in mock chagrin. "You cowboys are so chauvinistic. That's the same way you sounded when you took Matthew out to see Goliath."

He brushed his fingers over her breasts. "Believe me, sweetheart, I feel a great deal differently toward you than I do that bull." His eyes glittered with lascivious intent. "After the dance you're coming back to the ranch with me."

"Yes."

"I want you in my bed. Warm. Naked. Mine."

This time she was unable to resist his unmistakably possessive tone. "Yours," she whispered, knowing as she said the word that there could be no turning back.

The parking lot of the Grange was almost full when Molly cautiously parked next to a red pickup. The bumper sticker on the Dodge truck proclaimed the driver to be a Roper, Not a Doper. Having never driven anything that equaled the sleek black automobile in speed or power, she had always considered men's love affairs with sports cars rather silly. Tonight she fully understood the lure. It was power, pure and simple. And power, she had discovered, was a potent aphrodisiac.

Cole had watched Molly with amusement, wondering if she realized that her face constantly mirrored her thoughts. She'd enjoyed driving the car. Strange that such a simple thing could give her so much pleasure. He wished he'd thought of it earlier.

"I think I made a big mistake tonight," he said as she turned off the engine with a regretful little sigh.

"Mistake?" Molly ran her fingertips over the steering wheel, as if reluctant to give up possession quite yet.

He grinned. "You look just like you do after we make love," he said. "Warm, flushed, satisfied." He ran his fingers down her face. "I'd hate to think I could be replaced by a car. Even a Ferrari."

Molly's eyes gave him her answer first. "Never."

He leaned toward her, intent on capturing those softly smiling lips when a large hand slapped the top of the car. "Hey, Cole," a masculine voice called out, "you're missing all the fun."

"That's what he thinks," Cole muttered. His gaze swept over her face. "You are exquisite."

Molly grinned. "You're not so bad yourself, cowboy."

There was a slight stir of interest when Molly and Cole entered together, but people soon returned to their conversations.

When a tall, husky man wearing worn denim, worlds away from the glitter of the Nashville scene, began singing a plaintive tale of the dangers of falling in love with a two-timing woman, it crossed Molly's mind that her mother had undoubtedly worked in many places a great deal like this. She closed her eyes tightly, vowing not to think about Loretta. For just this one night she was going to be selfish. She was going to think only of herself. And Cole.

"I love it here," Molly said as she and Cole began to dance to the slow ballad.

Cole looked around the room, taking in the knotty pine-paneled walls. "Most women'd probably be happier in the ballroom of a five-star hotel." When Molly tilted her head back to give him an impatient look, Cole shook his head. "Sorry. I'd forgotten we'd already determined that you are not most women."

"That's better." She rested her cheek on his shoulder once again. "It's a different world out here," she explained. "People are independent, self-sufficient. I like that."

The two words described Molly, as well. Cole figured that growing up in an orphanage had probably been responsible for her developing those particular character traits. Considering that he'd never met a woman more capable of standing on her own two feet, he decided that this was as good a time as any to bring up a subject he'd been putting off for weeks. "Your contract's up for renewal next month."

He didn't know what he was going to do if she went back to Chicago. For months he'd been telling himself that if Molly chose not to stay, all he'd be losing was one helluva good teacher. The past week had forced him to admit that a great deal more was at stake.

Maybe he could just hog-tie her until she agreed to sign on the dotted line. No, Cole decided, that was too drastic a measure. He'd have to handle this like the shrewd businessman he was reputed to be. First he'd appeal to her sense of responsibility toward her students. If that didn't work, he'd try seducing her into acquiescence. If those methods failed, *then* he'd tie her up.

Molly heard the forced casualness in Cole's tone and wondered if he was about to inform her that she wouldn't be offered a contract to teach next year. She'd known it was foolish to get involved with anyone who had such power over her life. If Cole ever tired of her, he could fire her without a backward glance.

She might not have minded so much if she hadn't come to love this community—the land and the people, especially the kids. They were special and, in turn, they made her feel special. She'd felt as if she belonged here the moment she'd arrived, and the past six months had only reinforced that feeling.

"That's right," she murmured, matching his casual tone. "I'd nearly forgotten."

His fingers played with the soft blond waves skimming down her back. "You know, of course, that the board wants you to stay."

"And you?" She tried to sound nonchalant.

"I think that should be obvious."

Molly could feel the relieved grin spreading across her face. "I think I'd like to hear it."

He tugged lightly on the ends of her hair, encouraging her to look up at him. "I want you to stay, Molly."

She leaned against him deliberately and linked her hands behind his neck. "Then it's unanimous. Because I want to stay."

Relief was instantaneous. Cole's hands moved down her back, following the curve of her buttocks as he pressed her against the lower half of his body. He bent his head and took Molly's mouth with a slow, forceful hunger that left her trembling.

"What are you doing this summer?" he asked idly as he stroked the small of her back.

Molly's mind was floating on a gilt-edged cloud. "I don't know. I thought I'd catch up on my reading, lie in the sun, plant a garden. Why?"

"I've got a job offer for you."

"Working for you?"

"I knew you were a clever lady."

"Doing what?" she asked suspiciously. If he dared ask her to be his mistress, she was going to slap his face, even if everyone within a fifty-mile radius had shown up here tonight.

"The same thing Randy wants to do for the Circle L."

"You want a history of the Double Diamond?"

"I've been thinking about it for a long time," he said. "Up until now I'd never met anyone capable of putting it together. There are a lot of old letters, journals, documents, photographs, that sort of thing, stored in boxes all over the house. And of course a lot of the hands have worked there all their lives, so they've got some stories to tell, as well. It'd be a tough job, but—"

"I'd love it," Molly said immediately, her mind already whirling with possibilities. She kissed him again, quick and hard. "I can hardly wait."

He smiled at her dancing eyes. "Don't you want to know how much it pays?"

"Of course I don't," she returned with a grin. "How much?"

He mentioned an amount that made her stare up at him. "Cole, that's far too much."

"No, it's not. Nobody's ever sorted that stuff out, Molly. It's going to be one helluva job. If you want to know the truth, you're probably being underpaid. Oh, and of course it comes with room and board."

"Room and board? But I won't be staying at the ranch, Cole. I've already told you that."

The song ended and was replaced by a toe-tapping, fast-paced bluegrass number. As Molly and Cole wended their way back to their table, Cole reminded himself to be patient. Molly reminded him more and more of Gypsy, his palomino quarter horse. Gypsy had been born flighty, and more than one old hand had wagered that he'd never be able to gentle her. And if he'd followed the lessons of the old school, their predictions probably would have been true. Cole had never been a proponent of breaking a horse, of riding it until it was too tired or too confused to resist.

Instead, he'd taken his time with Gypsy, gaining the filly's confidence. His first steps had been a lot of touching and handling, letting the horse know that she had nothing to fear from him. The time had paid off; Gypsy did what he wanted her to do because she wanted to please him, not because she was afraid.

Although he knew she'd be infuriated by the comparison, Cole didn't want to break Molly's spirit. He wouldn't have been interested in her if she'd been a meek, acquiescent female. No, he enjoyed watching those flares of temper almost as much as he enjoyed sampling the more pleasurable aspects of her passionate nature. Over the past weeks he had decided that he wanted Molly as much for her strength as for her softness. The trick, Cole considered, would be to coax her into staying at the ranch because she wanted to. Not because he was insisting on it.

"It's not what you think," he said as he signaled the waitress for two beers. "You'd have your own room." As much as Cole hated the idea, he realized it was important to make the offer.

Molly studied him with a wary look that once again brought Gypsy to mind. "I would?"

"Of course. As much as I'd like to move you into my bed, I accept your feelings, Molly. I won't push for anything you're not ready to give."

Personally, Molly thought it was Cole who was avoiding opening up to everything their relationship could be, but she decided this was neither the time nor the place to bring that up. "If you really feel that way, why bother having me stay at the ranch?"

"In the first place, it's no bother. Dallas is used to cooking for the crew, so one more mouth, even one as delectable as yours—" he traced the full line of her lips tenderly with his finger "—isn't going to make a difference."

"And in the second place?"

"This isn't going to be an eight-to-five job, Molly. If you're staying at the ranch, it'll be easier to set your own pace. Besides, you won't be able to interview the men until evening, and it's a long drive back to your house."

She had to admit the idea had merit. "I'd want to keep my room at the house so I'd have a place to live when school starts again."

Cole could accept that. He'd already gotten what he wanted and with a lot less trouble than he'd expected. "Agreed. So do we have a deal?"

The waitress had returned with their order, and Molly raised her icy mug to his. "It's a deal."

Cole grinned as if he had never doubted the outcome. "Terrific. Wait and see, Molly Fairchild, we're going to make a great team."

As Molly thought about compiling the history of the Double Diamond, a new idea began to take shape in her mind.

"Cole, I've just had the most brilliant idea."

He lifted their linked hands and brushed his lips over her knuckles. "Me, too. Let's go home."

She smiled, very tempted by the way he was looking at her. "I was thinking about the school," she admitted.

"The school." He laughed at that. "I should have guessed it when I saw that wild light in your eyes." He sighed as he pressed a kiss against the inside of her wrist. It looked as if it were going to be a long evening. "How much is this brilliant idea going to cost? What with all your little projects, like the magazine and the theater, Barbara's microwave oven and Mike's computer, you three are turning out to be the most expensive teachers of the bunch. I'm beginning to think we never should have arranged for you to room together. What do you do—stay up nights thinking of ways to spend more of the school's money?"

His voice was cheerful, so Molly decided not to take offense at his words. "This won't cost you a thing," she promised. "Well, maybe a bit. In the beginning," she admitted as he raised his brows in challenge. "But I know we'll be able to recoup all our losses. In fact," she said, her enthusiasm increasing, "we'll probably even make a profit."

"I'll believe that when I see it."

He wondered if she realized how beautiful she was when she was waxing enthusiastic about her work and decided that she didn't. Molly's ingenuousness was one of her most charming traits. It made a man consider things he'd always believed impossible—like a wife, kids. . . .

Cole belatedly realized that Molly was talking a mile a minute. Blinking away the romantic images, he struggled to catch up with her.

"So," she finished up with a satisfied smile, "we'll have the same printer who does the magazine put it together and we'll sell it by mail order all over the state. What do you think?"

"About what?"

"The book, of course."

"Book?"

"Each student will write a short history about his family's past, then we'll bind them together and market the book as a history of Oregon's settlers.... Were you listening to anything I said?"

"I was. But then I got sidetracked watching your lips. You're a remarkably beautiful woman, Molly."

The quiet words, the intensity in his eyes, momentarily threw her off balance. "I think you've just redeemed yourself," she said finally.

He grinned, feeling worlds better and years younger than he had in ages. "I'm glad. By the way," he murmured as they walked back toward the dance floor, "you're right."

"About what?"

He dropped a light kiss on her lips. "It *is* a brilliant idea."

As she settled into his arms, Molly was irrationally happy.

It soon became apparent to everyone present that Cole Murdock had put his brand on Molly Fairchild. It wasn't that he threatened any man who might dare to ask her to dance; that wasn't Cole's style. Instead, his quiet air of possession as he remained steadfastly by Molly's side along with his obsidian-like eyes was enough to intimidate the most stalwart of potential admirers. Except one.

Molly and Cole were seated at their table when Randy Lawson appeared beside them. "Excuse me, Cole," he said, looking down at the toes of his oiled lizard-skin boots with obvious nervousness, "but would it be okay if I danced with Ms Fairchild?"

"Perhaps you should ask Ms Fairchild that question," Cole suggested reasonably.

The young man bit his lip as he dragged his gaze from the floor to Molly. His distressed brown eyes reminded her of a cocker spaniel's. "I'm not that good a dancer," he apologized. "But I'll try not to step on your feet."

Molly smiled as she rose from the table. "I'd love to dance with you, Randy."

"Gosh, thanks a lot, Ms Fairchild." Randy Lawson looked as if he'd just gotten a Christmas present eight months early. "Thanks, Cole," he flung back over his shoulder.

His hand was moist against Molly's as he moved stiltedly to the music. He was a great deal taller than she but painfully thin, although Molly knew he'd fill out in the coming years. When he did, he was going to be an extremely handsome young man, and she had no doubt that many young women in the county would be flinging themselves at him. Right now, however, he appeared to be painfully shy with the opposite sex; Molly had chaperoned several school parties and couldn't remember seeing Randy dance with any of the girls. And he'd certainly never shown up with a date. Remembering how feelings of inadequacy were such an integral part of her own teen years, Molly's heart went out to him.

"I got an acceptance letter from Oregon State today," he blurted out suddenly.

Molly tilted her head back and smiled up at him. "I knew you could do it."

"And Dad's agreed to let me go. In fact, he'd never admit it, but I think he might've actually been proud when that letter arrived."

Molly's heart melted as she looked up into his hopeful young face. Unable to resist, she put her hand briefly on his cheek. "I'm sure he was."

"I couldn't have done it without you."

"Of course you could have."

"No!" As his voice rang out and several nearby couples turned around to look at them, Randy's face turned beet red. "No," he repeated, his voice lower but every bit as firm. "I never would have even imagined going to college if you hadn't brought it up. You were the one who encouraged me to dream, Ms Fairchild. And then you made the dream come true."

"You made the dream come true, Randy. With all your hard work. And your talent."

He shook his head emphatically. Hair the color of ginger fell across his freckled brow. "That's not true. It was all your doing." His slender fingers tightened on hers. "I love you, Ms Fairchild."

Molly knew that Randy's mother had died five years ago when he was twelve, an impressionable age. Although it had been obvious that in the beginning Randy had viewed her as a mother figure, Molly had been aware that his feelings had begun to shift into something more romantic during the past few months as they'd worked together on the college project. Although she had been careful to remain professional at all times, she couldn't deny that she'd grown to care deeply for the intense, motherless boy.

"I love you, too, Randy. Although teachers aren't really supposed to have favorites, every once in a while a student comes along who's so special we really can't help ourselves."

His expression became earnest. "That's not what I mean," he insisted. "You don't understand. I *love* you. Really love you."

"Randy—"

"If you're worried about the difference in our ages, everyone says that I'm really mature for seventeen." He continued to press his case eagerly. "Besides, once I get out of college, I'll be twenty-one and you'll be what, twenty-five, twenty-six? That's hardly any difference at all."

"I'll be thirty," she corrected softly. "And you're right, age doesn't matter when you're in love. But the truth is, there are a lot of different ways to love a person, Randy, and I don't love you in the way you're talking about."

"You could try."

"No," she insisted gently, "I couldn't. Because I already care for someone very deeply."

"Cole," he grumbled.

Molly nodded. "That's right."

"Dammit, it's just not fair. Cole hadn't paid any attention to you until that day he came to our class." The music had stopped and they were standing in the center of the dance floor. "I've loved you forever, Molly!"

Seeing the pain and frustration in his eyes, Molly felt as if her heart were being ripped to ribbons. "Randy, you don't understand," she began, placing her hands on his arms.

"Oh, I understand." He fiercely jerked free of her light touch. "I understand I made a damned fool of myself. So what else is new?" He stormed away, out into the night.

Molly was following him when Cole caught her arm. "Let him go," he advised mildly. "He needs to be alone right now. Besides, the fresh air'll cool him down."

Knowing that his suggestion had merit, Molly sank down at their table and pressed her fingertips wearily against her temples. "I can't say that I didn't see it coming," she admitted. "I just didn't know what to do about it."

"There wasn't really anything you could have done, sweetheart. Randy will just have to learn it's all part of growing up. None of us manages to pull it off without a few scars."

"I suppose you're right." She sighed. "Lord, I wouldn't go back to being his age for anything in the world."

"I doubt if there's anyone out there who would. And if it's any consolation, the kid will wake up someday and realize how lucky he was that his first love was someone who sincerely cared for him." He took her hand in his, lifting her fingers to his lips. "It makes a difference, Molly."

As opposed to her immature crush on David? And Cole's ill-fated marriage to Laura? Looking at it that way, Molly felt immeasurably better. "You're so good for me," she said softly, her green eyes filled with uncensored love as they met his.

"Sweetheart, the feeling's mutual," Cole returned with emotion.

As the night wore on, the music, along with the level of conversation, grew increasingly lively. Bells and buzzers from a pair of old-fashioned pinball machines in the corner added to the cacophony. Cowboys, deprived of their usual snuff, had begun to smoke, creating a thick blue haze that hovered over the dancers.

Two brief skirmishes broke out, but both were settled reasonably peacefully out in the parking lot. Although the night air was still cool, the temperature in the crowded room had risen several degrees by eleven o'clock. Molly excused herself, escaping through a door labeled Heifers.

Running water into the sink, Molly dampened a paper towel from the stack on the counter and pressed it against her throat. "Boy, did I ever need that," she murmured as she held the cool towel to the back of her neck.

"What you need," a feminine voice said tartly, "is to go back to Chicago. Where you belong."

Molly slowly lifted her gaze to the mirror. Marlene Young was leaning against the wall, her dark eyes glittering with malevolence. She was wearing a red silk Western shirt, open at the neck to reveal a deep triangle of tanned flesh. Her black jeans looked as if they'd been spray-painted on, displaying a trim body that Molly knew was the result of hard physical work. Her black hair shone like ebony as it fell straight to the middle of her back. She looked, Molly decided, like one of the thoroughbreds she raised on her Bar Y ranch. Sleek, strong and expensive.

"I like it here," Molly answered mildly.

Marlene pulled out a cigarette, lighting it with a slim silver lighter studded with turquoise stones. "Now that doesn't really matter, does it?"

"It does to me." Molly briefly thought back to the female fight scenes in all the old-time Westerns and wondered if she were about to gain firsthand experience. The idea, as unappealing as it sounded, made her smile.

"Something funny?" Marlene asked as she exhaled a cloud of smoke.

Molly shook her head. "Not really. I was just thinking about a John Wayne movie I saw a long time ago."

"That's the trouble with you city people," the other woman said, waving her cigarette. "You think life out here is like something from the movies."

"I'm not a city person, Marlene. I'm originally from a little town in West Virginia."

"Well, West Virginia sure as hell isn't cattle country," Marlene pointed out. "So it's the same thing. You're an outsider, lady. You'll always be an outsider. Why don't you just pack up and leave?"

"Isn't this where you tell me this town isn't big enough for the two of us?" Molly tossed the paper towel into the wastebasket. "I'll leave, when and if I'm ready. And not a moment before."

She was on her way out the door when Marlene's hand curled around her arm. As her fingers dug into Molly's flesh, Molly understood how such a slender woman could control two thousand pounds of unruly horseflesh. The woman had the grip of a world-class weight lifter.

"If you're hanging around here because of Cole Murdock, you're wasting your time," Marlene warned through gritted teeth. "Everyone's known for years that Cole and I are going to get married. His daddy and mine worked it out so the Double Diamond and the Bar Y could be joined together."

"Interesting how everyone forgot to tell Cole about this master plan," Molly said, deciding not to give the woman the pleasure of trying to get away. At least not until things began to look really dangerous.

"Cole married the wrong kind of woman once," Marlene spat out. "Believe me, he won't make the same mistake twice." She smiled, but the laughter didn't reach her cold, dark eyes. "Funny how the Murdock men have to learn the hard way, isn't it? First his daddy married that woman who took off when Cole was still running around in diapers, then he turned around and did the same damned thing." Her fingers tightened as she leaned closer. "But he's gotten that out of his system. When he marries again, it's going to be to one of his own kind."

If there was one thing Molly knew with certainty, it was that Cole wouldn't stand for anyone making his decisions for him. Not his father. And not Marlene Young.

"You know," Molly drawled softly, "since coming here to cattle country, I've become well acquainted with manure." She smiled engagingly. "But I don't believe I've ever encountered quite so much of it in one place."

Plucking the woman's fingers from her arm, Molly left the rest room. She'd never stooped to fighting over a man before, partly because she had never met one worth the effort. Including David. Mostly, however, Molly had always considered such behavior not only beneath her, but also degrading to women in general. But as she rejoined Cole at the table, she had to admit that the expression on Marlene Young's face had definitely been worth it.

11

MOLLY AWOKE THE FOLLOWING morning with a slow smile, a long stretch and a momentary disorientation that gave way to anticipation. Although there were still several weeks left before summer vacation, she'd planned to get an early start on the history of the ranch. She couldn't wait to begin.

She was neither surprised nor disappointed to find herself alone in the wide, comfortable four-poster bed where Cole's grandmother had given birth to his father. Cole had warned her, right before they'd finally drifted off to sleep, that he'd be branding cattle in the south section. The work, she knew, began at dawn.

Molly glanced over at the clock on the bedside table. It wasn't yet seven-thirty; if she hurried, she'd be able to watch the men work for a while before settling down to her own task. The idea of watching Cole in his element was undeniably appealing. She dressed quickly in the jeans and shirt she'd picked up from her house on the way back to the ranch after the dance.

As she walked across the expanse of dirt separating the house from the corral, Molly caught sight of Cole. He was astride Gypsy, cutting the calves from the herd, as his father had done and his father before him. As she watched, Molly realized that it wasn't only the men who were eager to engage the spirited animals in battle, but their horses, as well. Gypsy had positioned herself between one bull calf and his mother, and her dark eyes and nostrils dilated as she dared the calf to make his move. Each time the calf feinted, Gypsy shifted. The palomino seemed to second-guess the calf, always knowing which way he was going to move.

Molly caught her breath as the cow, frustrated by the separation, suddenly charged the horse. Responding to the pressure of Cole's left spur, Gypsy swirled around, easily avoiding the treacherous horns. When the calf took this opportunity to dash under Gypsy's neck, the graceful horse seemed to defy gravity, jumping in front of him to move him still farther away from the herd. A cowboy working on foot chased the defeated calf into the pen that held the calves already separated. Head erect, Gypsy snorted, awaiting her next challenge.

After the calves were separated, the men worked quickly with a red-hot iron, a knife and a needle. Stumbling to their feet, the branded and dehorned calves shook their heads, spraying blood on the cowboys before rejoining the herd where they were met by the anxious cows. One especially vocal animal was met by his mother, who licked him all over, obviously searching for wounds. Then she turned and glared at the cowboys, bawling angrily. Molly couldn't help feeling strangely empathetic.

The patches of grass became spattered with blood, the earth around the men matted and littered with horns as every minute or so they'd release another calf. Although Molly's stomach had initially done its share of flip-flops at the smell of burning cowhide, blood and medicine, as the sun rose higher in the sky, she remained perched on the top rail of the fence, unable to tear herself away from the grueling scene.

When they finally broke for dinner, Cole came over to her. "Well, you can't say that you haven't seen me at my worst now," he said, taking off his hat and running his fingers through his damp hair.

Molly observed him thoughtfully. The man who had wielded that knife so expertly was a far cry from the gray-suited cattleman who had taken her dancing last night. His damp, dust-covered shirt clung to his body, and sweat had left trails in the grime on his face. The sharp scent of his skin was strangely intoxicating.

Recalling what Marlene had said about the previous Murdock wives, Molly wondered if this had been when they first realized they were not cut out for ranch living. As her gaze returned to Cole's face, Molly found his dark eyes strangely watchful, as if her response was inordinately important.

She took her time in answering. "If you want to know the truth, on a very primitive level I'm beginning to understand why cowboys play a starring role in so many women's fantasies."

Something that appeared to be relief flooded into his eyes, replaced almost immediately by that wicked gleam Molly knew would still have the power to thrill her when she was ninety. "Primitive, huh?"

"Definitely."

He arched a brow. "I take it that's good?"

She touched her index finger to her lips before pressing it against his smiling mouth. "If you're still interested after you're done torturing all those baby cows, I'm willing to demonstrate exactly how good that is."

"It's a date," he agreed instantly, wondering what it was about Molly that could make him feel so damned good.

His body ached—over the past week he had discovered muscles he'd forgotten he had—and he was exhausted from last night's lack of sleep. But looking at her sparkling green eyes made Cole feel like an oversexed teenager.

He bent his head and kissed her. The kiss wasn't long, nor was it particularly passionate, but that didn't stop the cowboys from hooting their approval.

"We should be finished by three-thirty or four," he promised, his eyes drifting down to those soft, pliant lips that he knew he'd never get enough of.

Molly nodded. "I'll be waiting."

HER BLISSFUL MOOD evaporated the moment she returned home from the Double Diamond later that evening. "That hospital called again," Barbara announced as Molly entered the kitchen. "I'm all for helping my fellow man, but don't you think you're overdoing the charitable contribution bit, Molly?"

"It takes a lot of money to run a hospital," Molly murmured.

"Sure it does," Barbara agreed as she returned to stirring the thick beef stew she was preparing. "But what are you trying to do? Get a wing named in your

honor? You've been sending them practically your entire paycheck every month."

She shook the wooden spoon. "Personally, I think it's
time to find a new charity. And cut these guys off."

Molly hated deception. It made her feel cold. Sick.
Even now she could feel the beginnings of a killer
headache throbbing at her temple. "This is really none
of your business," she snapped.

Barbara looked surprised but, apparently deciding
that discretion was the better part of valor, failed to
comment on Molly's outburst. "Dinner'll be in twenty
minutes," she announced calmly. "I was just about to
make the dumplings."

"Twenty minutes," Molly agreed flatly. She headed
toward the back stairs leading up to the bedrooms, then
stopped. "Barb, I'm sorry. I had no right to bite your
head off that way."

Barbara lifted her shoulders in an elegant shrug. "We
all have bad days." As she turned back toward Molly,
her eyes were filled with sympathy. "Want to talk about
it?" she asked quietly. "The dumplings can wait."

Molly knew she wasn't fooling Barbara. The woman
would have had to be blind or stupid not to notice that
Molly got upset whenever one of those mysterious letters or telephone calls came from the Charleston, West
Virginia, hospital. And Barbara was neither. What she
was was a friend. One who might not be able to fully
empathize with her problem, but who could provide a
sympathetic ear, which Molly suddenly needed. Desperately.

Personal revelations had never been easy for Molly. She had created a colorful, but sanitized story of her childhood, one that was becoming more and more difficult to sustain. "It's complicated," she began slowly, wondering where to start.

Unfortunately, Mike chose that precise moment to burst in the screen door. "I could smell dinner a block away," he announced with a broad grin. "So when do we eat?"

Barbara's eyes didn't leave Molly's pale face. "Later."

But the moment had been lost, and both women knew it. Molly pasted a forced smile on her face as she turned toward Mike. "Twenty minutes," she assured him. "Barbara was starting to make the dumplings. Let me make a quick phone call and I'll be back down to set the table."

After she had left the room, Barbara slammed her spoon down on the counter and whirled around to glare at Mike. "I've half a mind to dump this stew right over your head."

His confused gaze went from Barbara to the stew to the deserted stairway before returning to Barbara's glittering blue eyes. "Oh-oh," he muttered, dragging his hand down over his face. "Another call?"

"That's right," Barbara confirmed. "And I was about to get to the bottom of things when you came bursting in the door like some ill-mannered five-year-old. Haven't you ever heard of knocking?"

"In my own house?"

Barbara didn't bother answering. Her mind was upstairs, with a frustratingly closemouthed Molly Fairchild.

Molly sat on the edge of her bed, her back ramrod straight, her ice-cold fingers curled around the telephone receiver. When the voice on the other end told her what she already knew, she inclined her head.

"Yes," she said quietly, realizing that the nod was useless over the long-distance wires. "Yes, I understand that you've done everything possible. Yes, I realize that it's difficult."

She shut her eyes briefly. *Don't you think it's been difficult for me?* she wanted to cry out. But Molly had never been one to wallow in self-pity and she wasn't going to begin now.

"I assume you called the sheriff," she continued, her voice regaining its usual steady tone. Of course they had. Everyone had the routine down pat after all these years. Including her. "I'll call Mr. Pence." Molly nodded again. "Yes, I'll be waiting for your call."

She hung up and immediately dialed Billy Joe's number. Her fingers tapped nervously on the bedside table as she listened to the telephone ring. And ring. And ring. Finally, just as she was about to hang up, his familiar voice answered.

"H'llo?"

"She's gone again," Molly said without preamble. She pressed her fingers against her closed lids and nodded while he calmly proceeded to reassure her as he always did. "One of these days, Billy Joe Pence," she declared fervently, "I'm going to find a way to make all this up to you."

Despite Billy Joe's best intentions, his encouraging words did little to restore Molly's spirits.

As APRIL SHOWERS ushered in bright May flowers, Molly found herself unable to remember a world without Cole in it. Although their work kept them apart a great deal of the time, the hours they managed to steal together were the happiest she had ever known.

The only cloud on the horizon was Loretta, who seemed to have dropped off the face of the earth. Every so often, when she was too relaxed to fully control her emotions, Cole saw a sad little shadow move across Molly's face. When he asked about it, she offered some pale excuse, knowing that she should tell him the truth. That he, of all people, would understand.

Molly had always been pragmatic; life had taught her at an early age that people who make the mistake of dreaming about happily-ever-afters only end up being disappointed. Until now, until Cole, she had never known exactly how seductive happiness could be. And despite a stab of guilt each time she invented a reason for her momentary depression, Molly couldn't bear the thought of reality cruelly intruding on her blissful world. So she held her tongue, vowing each day that she would tell him tomorrow. Or the next day. *Soon*, she continued to promise herself as the halcyon, sun-warmed days grew increasingly longer.

They were two weeks away from the end of the school year when a tragic reality reared its ugly head and shattered the fantasy. Molly was at the school, planning the upcoming commencement ceremonies with the graduation committee. The meeting was coming to a close when Cole suddenly appeared in the doorway, his hat in his hand. Molly's warm greeting trailed off when she saw his grim expression.

"What's the matter?" she asked, hurrying over to him.

She was so slender, Cole marveled as he took hold of her shoulders. So fragile. Although he knew Molly possessed a deep inner strength, he also realized that she was more vulnerable than she cared to admit. As he looked down into her troubled eyes, Cole was struck with a fleeting urge to protect her. To lie.

"It's Randy."

Cooling relief that he hadn't brought bad news about her mother was immediately overcome by a dark, sinking dread. Although Randy had remained decidedly remote toward her since the debacle at the Cattlemen's Association dance, Molly could not have cared more for him if he'd been a member of her own family.

"What about him?"

"His horse stepped in a gopher hole and fell on him, Molly," Cole told her gently. "It looks as if he's got a broken back. And some internal injuries."

"Oh, my God." Molly held on to Cole's shoulders to steady herself as she went suddenly light-headed. "Where is he?"

"They're flying him into Portland; he needs a trauma team. Matt's with him."

"We have to go," she insisted, grabbing her purse from the nearby table.

"I've already gassed up the plane."

"What about Lori?"

"Merle went over to the Circle L and got her," Cole revealed. "He and Dallas are with her now."

"Thank God for Dallas," Molly murmured, remembering all the times in her own life she'd cried out impotently for a mother who was never there. "Lori shouldn't be alone."

Not for the first time, Cole demonstrated that he and Molly were on the same wavelength. "Dallas and Merle might not have any kids of their own," he said. "But she's got a real natural gift for mothering. Lori'll be okay."

Time crawled by at a snail's pace as Cole piloted the Double Diamond's Cessna toward Portland. Sensing Molly's distress, he remained silent, leaving her to her frantic, unspoken prayers, reaching out periodically to squeeze her hand. She was not surprised to discover upon landing that Cole had already arranged for a rental car; she had learned long ago that he didn't forget even the smallest detail.

"He's going to be all right," he assured her as they made their way through rush-hour traffic.

"Of course he is," Molly agreed fervently. "After all, he's scheduled to give the valedictory next week. He wouldn't miss that opportunity, not after having worked so hard to earn those grades while working on the ranch. And don't forget college."

College. She refused to believe that her hard-won victory on Randy's behalf could be in vain. Molly had to push the words past the huge lump in her throat. "He's already paid his dorm deposit; Lori told me that he mailed it yesterday."

"He'll make it," Cole repeated firmly as he pulled into the parking lot of the University of Oregon Medical Center.

They found Matthew Lawson pacing in an empty waiting room, the lines on his weathered face deeper, harsher than usual. The ashtrays overflowing with cigarette butts told their own story.

"How is he?" Molly asked immediately.

"They've had him upstairs in surgery ever since we got here," Matthew replied with obvious frustration. "I haven't been able to get anyone to tell me a thing."

Cole put a comforting hand on his neighbor's shoulder. "He'll be all right, Matt. Randy's a tough kid."

"When I get back," Matt growled determinedly, "I'm going to shoot that damned horse."

"Oh, you can't do that," Molly protested.

His gray eyes had the hardness of flint. "And why the hell not?"

"Because Randy loves Shadow," she insisted. "He writes about him all the time. And he'll want to ride him as soon as he gets out of here."

Matt rubbed his chin. "You sure are one to look on the bright side, aren't you, Miz Fairchild?"

"I suppose I am, Mr. Lawson," she answered mildly.

His expression remained grim, but Molly thought she saw a softening in his eyes. "Suppose that's what Randy sees in you," he muttered finally. "You're a lot like the boy's mama. Mary was always lookin' for the silver lining."

"Mary was a wonderful woman," Cole said.

"She was that," Matt agreed morosely. "The Circle L just hasn't been the same since she passed on."

"I see a lot of her in Randy," Cole offered comfortingly. "The boy's got his mother's eyes. Her smile. And her zest for living."

"It's that spirit that's going to help him make it," Molly added firmly.

A glimmer of hope flickered in Matthew Lawson's red-rimmed eyes. "Think so?"

Molly and Cole both nodded. "I know so," they said in unison.

THE HOURS DRAGGED BY as they waited for some word of Randy's progress. Cole located a vending machine down the hall, but the coffee tasted like battery acid and the sandwiches could have been made from sawdust. But none of them had an appetite, anyway. The food went uneaten; the coffee was drunk only in lieu of anything stronger.

The nurses' shift changed. New nurses, their uniforms starched and clean, their manner brisk and efficient, came on duty. The waiting room where Molly, Cole and Matthew kept their vigil was next door to the emergency room; as the night wore on, business seemed to increase exponentially by the hour.

There were two muggings, one gunshot wound, three automobile accidents—one involving a motorcycle—

and a knife wound that was the result of a domestic squabble. All before midnight. But still there was no word of Randy.

A young woman arrived alone, obviously in the final stages of labor.

A couple carried in a pink-cheeked two-year-old, panic-stricken because their child had swallowed a penny. A well-dressed woman escorted by a man in a tuxedo arrived. Her left eye was swollen shut, the area around it already turning an ugly shade of purple. She'd been hit by a flying champagne cork, Molly overheard her husband tell the admitting nurse. The resident on duty had just begun to examine the woman's wound when a doctor, dressed in green scrubs, appeared in the doorway. He looked every bit as exhausted as Molly felt. Even worse, she decided.

"Mr. Lawson?"

Matthew pushed himself out of the chair. "That's me," he said, his voice unsteady.

"Your son is an incredibly strong-willed young man. We almost lost him twice, but he managed to fight his way back each time."

"Randy's always been single-minded," Matthew agreed gruffly, exchanging a significant glance with Molly.

"Well, it's lucky for all of us that he is. That horse didn't do him any favors."

"How's my boy now?" Matthew asked anxiously. "Can I see him?"

"He's still in recovery," the doctor explained. "After he comes out of the anesthetic, we'll be moving him to

ICU, where we can keep a close eye on him. As for his injuries, we fused the broken vertebrae together and he should be able to walk, but he may have a tendency to drag his right leg. Physical therapy can help with that. Once upon a time I would've predicted your son wouldn't ride again, but last year there was a kid in here who'd sustained much the same injury while bareback riding and he's back on the rodeo circuit. In fact, he came in last week and gave me the buckle he'd just won, so I wouldn't count anything out on that score."

The exhausted, middle-aged man smiled for the first time since entering the room. "One thing I learned long ago is that kids are tough. They'll surprise you every time."

"Then Randy's going to be all right?" Cole inquired.

The doctor's smile faded as his expression turned cautious. "To tell you the truth, I can't promise anything at this point. Randy had internal injuries, and he lost a great deal of blood. The next twelve to twenty-four hours will tell the story. If he survives those, I'd say he's got a good chance for a full recovery." His intelligent gray eyes moved over the weary threesome. "I'm about to go home and get some sleep. I'd suggest you all do the same."

"I'm stayin' here," Matthew insisted. Randy might have inherited his mother's eyes and smile, but Matthew's outthrust chin demonstrated precisely where the boy had gotten his tenacity.

"Really, Mr. Lawson, there isn't anything you can do here," the doctor protested.

Matthew folded his arms across his broad chest. "I'm stayin'."

The weary doctor rubbed his face with his hand. "Far be it from me to argue. Good night, Mr. Lawson, I'll see you in the morning. If there's anything you need, just ask one of the nurses." With that he was gone.

"Cole and I are staying, too," Molly said as they all settled back down on their hard vinyl chairs.

Matt studied her thoughtfully. "I'm not so sure that's a good idea, Miz Fairchild. No offense, ma'am, but you look as if you'd been rode hard and put away wet."

"Matt's right, Molly." Cole seconded Matthew's opinion, despite his less-than-flattering description. "You look dead on your feet, sweetheart. I think we ought to find you some place to lie down."

Molly could feel them ganging up on her and wasn't about to allow it. Sure, she was a little tired. But who wouldn't be after what they'd been through? Not to mention the sleepless nights she'd spent tossing and turning the past couple of weeks, waiting for the phone to ring, waiting for news of Loretta.

"That's ridiculous," she protested. "I'm perfectly fine. And I'm not leaving Randy."

"You're not going to be able to see him, anyway," Cole pointed out.

"Then I'm not leaving Mr. Lawson."

Matthew squatted in front of her, his gray eyes gentle in his careworn face. "Nothin' personal, Miz Fairchild, but I'd kinda like some time to myself."

"Well . . . if you're sure," she said hesitantly.

Matthew nodded emphatically. "I'm sure."

"All right." As she agreed to some rest, Molly suddenly realized just how exhausted she was. She felt like a dishrag, wrung out and left on the line to dry. "And after all we've been through tonight, Mr. Lawson, I think you'd better call me Molly."

He managed a smile. "You got yourself a deal, Molly. And I'm Matt."

She inclined her head. "He *is* going to be fine, Matt," she said softly.

"I didn't believe that in the beginning," he admitted gruffly. "But, you know, I'm startin' to think you might just be right about this one, too. There's a chapel down the hall. I saw it when they first brought Randy in. I haven't set foot in a church since Mary died, but right now I kinda feel like doing some heavy-duty praying."

"You won't be alone, Matt," Cole promised.

THEY REFRAINED FROM TALKING as Cole drove to a nearby hotel. Soon Molly, stripped down to her underwear, sank thankfully onto the king-size mattress in their room.

"I guess I'm more tired than I thought," she admitted.

"Perhaps we should have had a doctor check you out while we were at the hospital," he reflected as he sat down on the edge of the bed and ran his hand down her arm.

"Don't be ridiculous," she murmured drowsily. "All I need is a little sleep. I'll be as good as new in a couple of hours."

Hoping that she was right, Cole took off his clothes. He tenderly covered Molly, then slid under the covers and wrapped his arm around her shoulders, pulling her against him. Molly snuggled up to him, fitting her soft curves to his hard male frame. She fell asleep instantly, and he could feel the soft sigh of her breath against his chest.

As he pressed a soft kiss on the top of her head, Cole could feel the tension of all those aggravating hours of waiting gradually seeping out of him, and with it came an awareness of his own fatigue. He was on the brink of sleep himself, but there was one more thing left to do.

It had been a very long time since Cole Murdock had prayed for anyone or anything. He no longer remembered the words, so all he could do was state his case as simply and honestly as he knew how. Hoping that he might have at least earned a few points for sincerity, he finally closed his eyes and allowed himself to drift into a deep, dreamless sleep.

Cole had no idea how long he'd slept; the blackout draperies kept any hint of daylight from entering the room. But aware of something being wrong, he roused himself instantly to consciousness and reached out for Molly.

She was lying on the very edge of the bed, her eyes tightly closed and her shoulders heaving with sobs. "Molly?" Raising himself on one elbow, Cole brushed the tears away with his knuckles. "It's going to be all right, sweetheart. Randy's going to be fine."

"What if he isn't?" she whispered. "What if he dies?" The tears began flowing again, faster, harder. "Oh,

God," she cried out in a deep, tortured wail, "what if he dies before I ever get a chance to make amends for what I did to him?"

"Oh, sweetheart." Cole sat up, drawing her into his arms, running his fingers through her tousled, damp hair. "You haven't done anything to him. Except give him new horizons and bring a great deal of sunshine into his life."

Molly trembled violently as she pressed her cheek against his chest. "I . . . I . . . hurt him so badly," she sobbed painfully. "He loved me, Cole. And I handled it all wrong."

He stroked her back with a broad hand meant to soothe, not arouse. "You handled it the only way possible," he insisted. "You heard the doctor. Kids are tough, Molly. Randy's going to make it through this with flying colors, go on to college, then come home and give me a run for my money when he takes over the Circle L. And he's always going to remember you as the terrific lady who showed him the less traveled road."

"Oh, Cole, if only that were true." She clung to him, unnaturally cold, giving in to her almost overwhelming grief and fear. As he continued to caress her and murmur soft, consoling words, Cole felt as if his own heart were splitting in two.

After a while her weeping gradually ceased, and the tremors that had racked her slender body lessened. As Molly began to relax in his arms, Cole's caresses began to cause a slow, steady ache to build inside her. In response she began moving her hands up and down his back, exulting in the play of muscles beneath his flesh.

Cole tilted her head back so that he could look down into her face since his eyes had grown used to the dark. A soft blush suffused her cheeks, banishing last night's pallor. Her green eyes were eloquent pools of longing, and as they pulled him into their swirling depths, Cole felt as if he were drowning.

Kiss me. The words went unspoken, but Cole could read their message in Molly's love-softened eyes. "Yes," he murmured, bending his head. His mouth came down on hers as he lowered her slowly, gently back against the down-filled pillows. His lips plucked teasingly, tantalizingly at hers, moving from one corner of her mouth to the other and back again, as if he had all the time in the world and intended to savor every golden moment.

Touch me. His hands began a slow exploration of her body, his callused fingers never lingering in any one place too long as he proceeded to beguile her senses until Molly felt as if she were on the verge of melting. When his wide palms cupped her breasts and his thumbs rasped against her lace-covered nipples, a soft moan escaped Molly's throat.

"So smooth," he murmured, his clever, tantalizing hands skimming over her rib cage, across her taut stomach, lower and lower until they'd slipped past the elastic band of her bikini panties. "Your skin has always reminded me of silk." His fingers tangled for a brief, unsatisfactory moment in the blond thicket of curls at the apex of her thighs. "Satin. Velvet."

Love me. Molly's hips arched into the touch of his possessive hand, seeking release from the escalating heat within her. "Not yet," he murmured, his tongue teasing at her ear.

Molly was on fire. A thousand stinging, flickering flames licked at her nerve endings, and when his lips retraced the erotic path his hands had made, her body began to move insistently against his.

"Please, Cole," she whispered, caring little that she was begging, "I need you."

When she began stroking him, Cole almost surrendered to her feminine seduction. "I need you, too, sweetheart," he said with a ragged groan as he slipped away from her tender touch. "But just for now, for this one time, I want to make love to you first."

And he proceeded to do exactly that, his lips and hands and teeth making love to her in myriad ways, teasing, tasting, touching until she thought she'd go mad. He led her to the very brink of frenzy, over and over again, and then, when she knew she could take no more, he took her still further. Passion became unmanageable as she crested again and again, never quite catching her breath before Cole lifted her to a newer, higher peak. Her heart pounded, her blood roared, the movements of her body were wild and abandoned as she surrendered to a blazing inferno that threatened to engulf her.

Sensation after thrilling sensation slammed into her, and when Cole, unable to hold back any longer, surged into her welcoming softness, Molly began to weep once again. But this time the tears were not born of sorrow, but of love.

12

LATER—IT COULD HAVE BEEN minutes, hours or an eternity—Molly tried to move, only to find her leg trapped beneath Cole's. Deciding that she really didn't want to go anywhere, anyway, she lifted a languid hand and tenderly soothed the red welts her fingernails had created on his back.

"Mmm," Cole murmured against her throat, "that feels good." Lifting his head, he looked down at her, his eyes filled with lingering passion, gentle affection and something much more serious that Molly knew was echoed in her own.

"I love you," they said in unison.

Cole was amazed at how suddenly easy it was to say the words. "Love you," he said, kissing her chin, her cheeks. "Love you." His smiling lips trailed up her cheekbone. "Love you."

Molly laughed delightedly as his teeth lightly tightened on the delicate skin of her earlobe and tugged. "It's about time."

He raised an argumentative brow. "I didn't hear you rushing forward with any heated declarations."

"That's because I've been waiting for you."

"I see." He kissed her smiling lips. "And when did you come to this momentous decision?"

Molly ran her fingers through the crisp waves of his ebony hair. "I think I fell in love with you that first day in Chicago," she admitted. "I've just spent the rest of the time running away from reality."

He ran his hand down her side, delighting in the satiny feel of her skin under his fingertips. "I know the feeling all too well." He grinned down at her. "Feeling better?"

She pressed her palm against his cheek, which resembled the finest grade of sandpaper, and she shivered slightly at the memory of that morning beard against her heated flesh. "Thanks to you." Her soft smile faded. "I'm sorry about the tears, Cole, I don't usually fall apart like that."

"You're entitled, Molly. God knows, we all need a little help from time to time."

"I'll bet you don't."

"All of us," he insisted quietly.

The gentle expression on his face touched her deeply. "We'd better call the hospital," she said in an attempt to change the subject before it became unbearably personal.

"Or we could just go over there."

"No." She shook her head. "If anything bad has happened, I want a chance to regain control of myself before meeting Matt."

"No one expects you to always be in control, Molly," Cole said as he picked up the telephone.

"I do," Molly countered quietly.

Frustrated by Molly's behavior, but knowing that this was no time to argue the point, Cole dialed the hospital.

"Good news," he said as he hung up a few minutes later. "They've upgraded his condition from critical to serious."

Molly's expression was hopeful. "Does that mean he's out of the woods?"

"Not quite yet. But it's looking a lot better."

"How's Matt? Did you talk to him?"

"He's sleeping."

"On one of those horrid little chairs? How?"

"One of the nurses took pity on him around six this morning and put him to bed in a vacant room. Since Randy's condition had already changed, she was able to convince him that Randy would need all his father's support."

"Something he couldn't give when he was dead on his feet."

Cole smiled. "Exactly. I talked to the nurse; she said to give him another hour, hour and a half before we show up."

"What will we do for all that time?"

"Well, for a start, I suppose breakfast would be in order."

"You're determined to turn me into a breakfast person, aren't you?"

"I'm only thinking of you, babe," he said quietly.

Simple words, but they shook Molly to the core. All her life she had remained intensely independent, and it was only recently, only since her relationship with Cole began, that she realized her independence had been born more of a necessity than of desire.

The only person she had ever allowed to see her break down was Billy Joe. And even then she'd never allowed herself to weep uncontrollably in front of him as she'd done this morning with Cole. Not that she hadn't had plenty of reasons, thanks to Loretta's latest escapade.

As thoughts of her mother began to fill her with a cold, dark dread, Molly shut her eyes briefly, willing her premonition away. She could only handle one crisis at a time, and this morning it was Randy who needed her prayers and concern.

"I think I'll take a shower," she said finally.

Cole nodded. It had been there again, that strange sorrow that came over Molly from time to time. Her brief emotional collapse had left her drained—that much was obvious. But as the now familiar dark shadow moved across her face, Cole watched her body instinctively tense.

More and more he was coming to the conclusion that Molly was hiding something from him, and he vowed that once Randy was on the mend, they were going to get her secret out into the open. Because there wasn't anything she could tell him that could possibly change the way he felt about her.

"Good idea," he agreed encouragingly. "I'll order breakfast."

Molly had been aware of Cole's scrutiny. Relieved that he wasn't going to press her for answers now, she nodded, her eyes giving him her thanks before she escaped to the privacy of the bathroom.

Cole stared at the closed door for a long time. "Later," he promised under his breath. Then, with a deep sigh of resignation, he dialed room service.

"Feel like heading over to the hospital?" Cole asked after they'd finished breakfast. Although Molly had eaten halfheartedly, he was pleased to see that she'd at least made inroads in their stack of toast.

"You couldn't keep me away."

That there'd been a change in Randy's condition was obvious the moment they saw Matthew. His complexion, which had been a dark putty color last night, was ruddy. "Heard you called awhile ago," he greeted them with a grin.

"They gave us the good news," Cole assured him. "Not that I ever had any doubts," he hastened to add.

"I didn't, either," Molly lied emphatically.

Matthew turned to her. "The boy's been askin' for you."

"But he's in ICU." As much as Molly wanted to see Randy, she had no intention of risking his recovery to do so. "I didn't think they allowed visitors in intensive care."

"They don't, leastways most of the time. But he's been carryin' on so that the charge nurse decided it'd be easier to give you five minutes than to keep arguin' with him."

Molly's smile blossomed. "Five minutes," she promised.

Randy was in traction, various weights and pulleys keeping the strain off his back. He was on intravenous fluid, and assorted bandages and casts covered him. He looked dreadful. But as she considered how close they'd come to losing him, Molly decided that he looked wonderful.

"You had us all worried to death," she scolded him cheerfully as she approached his bed. "Your poor father must have gone through a carton of cigarettes last night."

"I keep telling him those things'll kill him," Randy said, managing something that almost resembled a smile.

"They're nearly as dangerous as getting in the way of a falling horse," Molly agreed.

"Dad said Shadow was all right."

There was a question in his tone, a question Molly hastened to answer. "Shadow's fine. He's just waiting for you to get back and exercise him."

"That'll be awhile," he said with a grimace.

"Better than not at all."

"I guess so." A significant silence hung between them.

"Randy—"

"Ms Fairchild—"

She smiled. "You first."

"About the night of the dance . . ."

Randy's expression was so earnest that it was all Molly could do not to give him an enormous hug. Instead, she tried to ease his mind. "Randy, we all say things we don't mean from time to time. It's human nature."

Obviously frustrated, he slapped his hand on the starched white sheet. "No. You don't understand."

Afraid of upsetting him further, Molly nodded. "I'm sorry. What were you saying?"

"I wanted to tell you that I wasn't making that up. I do love you, and whatever you say, I'm going to keep on loving you." Before Molly could respond, he continued. "The thing is, I've been giving it a lot of thought, and I understand that you love Cole. I can't say that I wouldn't rather have you fall in love with me, but if it has to be someone else, I'm glad it's him. He's a good man."

"He is that," Molly agreed softly.

"And since the Double Diamond and the Circle L are neighbors, at least we'll still be able to see each other. When I'm home for vacations."

"I can't think of anything I'd enjoy more," she said honestly.

"Then you don't mind?" he asked hesitantly, his eyes wide in his thin, pale face.

"Mind what?"

"That I love you?"

Molly covered his hand with hers. "Of course I don't mind," she said gently. "In fact, it's an honor to have someone as terrific as you feel that way about me." She gave him a warm, encouraging smile. "The girl who finally gets you, Randy Lawson, is going to be one lucky lady."

His pallid cheeks flushed crimson. "You're something else, Ms Fairchild."

"Thank you, Randy," Molly said easily. "You're not so bad yourself." She glanced up as the nurse appeared in the doorway. "I'd better go now before they throw me out." Bending, she brushed her lips against his cheek. "Get well soon. I've been looking for an excuse to throw a party."

Randy nodded. As Molly left the room, he lifted his hand to his cheek in silent wonder. Then, exhausted by the exchange, he fell asleep.

"WELL, THAT'S ONE WORRY taken care of," Cole said as they drove the rental car back to the airport. "Don't you think it's about time you filled me in on what's been bothering you?"

"Really, Cole," Molly protested, "I don't understand why you think anything's the matter."

"Because I know you," he said mildly. "And I love you. And a man'd have to be blind not to see that you've got something heavy working at your mind." He glanced over at her. "Burdens are a lot easier to carry if you share them, Molly."

Love. No matter how easily he said the word, Molly was all too aware that the emotion had not come easy for Cole. She knew it was foolish, but she couldn't make herself risk anything so new, so fragile.

"Then tell me about your problems," she insisted, gently nudging the conversation in another direction. "And why Matthew turned down your offer to stay here in Portland another few days because he knew you had to get back to the Double Diamond and straighten things out. What things?"

Cole shrugged, feeling his irritation level rise to new heights as Molly deftly sidestepped his question. "I've suspected that the ranch has been losing cattle," he said, giving up for the moment. "We were finally able to get an accurate count when we moved them to summer pasture."

"And?"

"We're six hundred short."

"Six hundred? That many?"

His expression was grim as he pulled up in front of the hangar. "That many."

As they flew back to the ranch, Molly kept thinking how difficult it must have been for Cole to be away from the Double Diamond at this time. Six hundred head of cattle missing was a very long way from a single rustler stuffing a lone calf into a Volkswagen. But not once had his worry over the stock stopped him from giving his concern for Randy and Matt top priority. Loyalty, Molly knew, was something Cole took very seriously. So why didn't she just tell him about Loretta and be done with it?

Pretending a sudden interest in the clouds floating past the windows of the plane, Molly took a deep breath, crossed her fingers and leaped into dangerous waters.

"Cole?"

"Yeah, honey?"

"I have something to confess."

At her words Cole struggled not to let the tension show on his face. "What's that?" he asked with deliberate casualness.

"I've lied to you."

He waited for the all too familiar distrust to come over him. When it didn't occur, Cole realized that the feeling had been banished by his love for Molly. "I find that difficult to believe," he said after a while.

"It's about my family."

"I didn't know you had any family," he said, confused by this latest twist. "I thought you grew up in an orphanage."

"I did. And foster homes when I got older. But I knew that you'd come to the conclusion that my parents were dead. And I never did anything to correct that impression."

"And they're not?"

"No. Well, maybe my father is," Molly admitted. "Since I've never known who he was, and I doubt that my mother did, either, he could be dead or alive for all I know."

"And your mother?"

"Has been an alcoholic for as long as I can remember. She gave me up shortly after I was born, but mountain people don't have any secrets from one another. I always knew Loretta Belle was my mother."

This was Molly's treacherous secret? The one that had been eating away at her? Relief washed over him. "Where's she now?"

"She's supposed to be in a hospital in Charleston, West Virginia, but she keeps running away." She dragged her fingers through her hair. "Oh, Lord, what a mess."

"Molly—"

"I'm sorry, Cole. I should have told you earlier."

"You should have told me," he agreed. "But only so I could have helped you through all this."

"Are you telling me that you actually would have fallen in love with me if you'd known that I was the bastard child of an alcoholic, failed country-and-western singer?"

There was a moment of stunned silence. "I can't believe you actually mean that," Cole said finally. "My God, Molly, the only lineages I care about are the ones belonging to my bulls." He reached out and covered her hand with his. It was ice-cold.

"I know it sounds silly," Molly murmured.

"And it is."

Her eyes misted with unshed tears as she finally met his infinitely patient gaze. "I love you," she whispered.

"And I love you," he affirmed. "More than I ever believed possible."

THE FINAL TWO WEEKS of school went by quickly, much to the relief of both faculty and students. Although it would be a long time before Randy was released from the hospital, the daily reports on his condition continued to be encouraging. Molly was pleased and interested when Karin Torgenson came into her classroom with the news that she'd been to visit Randy and he'd asked her to read his valedictory speech for him. Molly knew that Randy would likely have no room in his life for a serious relationship for several years, but she found the possibility of a budding romance between her two star students undeniably appealing.

Along with Loretta's continued disappearance another cloud began to loom on her horizon, a cloud that became darker with each passing day.

The afternoon after graduation Molly returned to the house she shared with Barbara and Mike. She had planned to spend the evening packing for her move to the Double Diamond, but now, as she sank into a wing chair in the living room, shock waves were still reverberating inside her head.

"It's about time you got home," Barbara said as she entered the living room with two glasses of champagne, one for herself and one for Molly. "We finally had to start the party without you."

Molly stared dumbly at the sparkling wine. "What are we celebrating? The end of the year?"

"My contract's been renewed," Mike announced proudly as he joined them.

"Congratulations."

"Hey, is that all you're going to say? Don't you know what a rare and special occasion this is? Not only have I broken a string of very unlucky encounters with school boards, but now Babs and I can get married."

Molly's stunned gaze went from Barbara to Mike and back again. "You're getting married?"

"Of course," Barbara said calmly. "That's what people in love usually do, isn't it?"

Molly's fingers slid up and down the crystal stem. "I suppose it is," she murmured. "I'm happy for both of you. Really, I am."

"You could say it like you mean it," Mike protested.

Barbara's blue eyes turned intense as she studied Molly's bleak expression. "Something's wrong. Is it something to do with your mother?"

Encouraged by Cole's response, Molly had broken down and confessed her secret to Barbara and Mike, as well. Both her friends had proven remarkably supportive as she had waited in vain for news about her mother.

Molly shook her head as she put the champagne, untouched, down on a nearby table. "No, I haven't heard from the hospital today, although Lord knows, with the way my luck is going, I probably will."

"Mike," Barbara suggested, giving him a pointed look, "why don't you go check the roast."

Molly made a vague gesture with her hand. "You might as well stay, Mike. Since pretty soon everyone in the county's going to know."

"Know what?" Barbara prompted gently.

Molly leaned her head against the back of the chair and briefly closed her eyes. "That I'm pregnant."

There was a brief moment of stunned silence. Barbara was the first to speak. "Are you sure?"

Molly nodded. "Positive. I had an appointment with Dr. Helbrose over in John Day this afternoon. She confirmed what I'd already begun to suspect."

"Hey," Mike said enthusiastically, "that's great, Molly. I've always wanted to be a godfather."

She opened her eyes to give him a long, weary look. "You don't understand."

"Understand what? That you're not married? Hell, Molly, Cole'll marry you the minute you tell him."

"That's precisely what I'm afraid of."

Both Barbara and Mike stared at her. "I thought you loved Cole," Barbara said finally.

"I do, but—"

"And it's obvious Cole loves you," Mike added.

"He says he does, but—"

"Cole would never say anything he doesn't mean, Molly," Mike insisted. "I'm a man. Believe me, I can tell when a fellow sufferer has it hard. Cole's wild about you."

"He also believes in truth. And loyalty. And responsibility," Molly said.

"Terrible traits in a man," Barbara agreed dryly. "I can see why you're concerned, Molly."

Leaning forward, her body a stiff, taut line, Molly tried to make her point. "Cole asked me about contraception very early on. I assured him I was on the pill."

"Were you?" Mike asked.

Molly shot him a brief, crushing glare. "Of course. I'd never lie about a thing like that."

"We didn't think you had," Barbara soothed, capturing Molly's hands as she twisted them in her lap. "So these things happen, honey. Cole will understand that."

"If he believes me."

"Why wouldn't he?"

"Because one of the major problems in our relationship from the beginning has been overcoming his distrust of women. Now just when I've managed to accomplish that enormous feat, I show up pregnant."

"He'll understand," Barbara assured her friend.

"Call Cole, Molly," Mike insisted. "Right now. Better yet, go out and see him. The sooner you get this off your chest, the better you'll feel."

"You're probably right." As Molly pushed herself out of the chair, Barbara and Mike exchanged a quick glance.

"Want a ride out there?" Mike asked.

Molly shook her head. "No, the drive will do me good. Clear my head." She turned in the doorway. "I'm so lucky to have both of you for friends."

Offering words of encouragement, Barbara and Mike embraced her warmly, then stood in the doorway until her car disappeared around the corner.

"Well, what do you really think?" Mike asked.

"It'll work out," Barbara decided. "As long as Molly doesn't mistake Cole's initial surprise for rejection.

She's always been so down-to-earth, I can't believe she's being so irrational."

"I've heard pregnancy makes a woman more emotional."

"Perhaps some women." Barbara's tone suggested she would certainly never fall prey to such ludicrous feelings.

"Think we should call Cole and warn him?"

She stared at him for a full ten seconds. "Sometimes you men absolutely floor me. Of course we're not going to call him to tell him anything this intimate. Besides, technically, it's none of our business."

"I sure wouldn't want to be kept in the dark while everyone else discussed my child's future," Mike complained.

Barbara kissed him. "Believe me, darling," she said silkily, "you'll be the very first to know."

DALLAS SENT SOMEONE OUT to find Cole the minute Molly arrived. If she observed the young woman with more than usual interest, she had the good sense to hold her tongue. Instead, she offered iced tea and cake, both of which Molly turned down.

"I think I'll just wait in the den."

"You do that, hon. Cole'll be along anytime."

Although the antique clock on Cole's desk told her that she'd only been waiting ten minutes, by the time he strode into the den, Molly was surprised she hadn't worn a groove in the wood floor.

"I tried to call you a few minutes ago," he said, wrapping his arms around her as he gave her a welcoming kiss. "But Barbara said you were already on your way out here."

"That's all?"

His lips grazed her cheeks. Soft, he thought. And sweet. If he lived to be a hundred, he'd never get over his luck. "All?" he asked absently, wondering if he had time to make love to Molly now before he left, and reluctantly decided he didn't.

"Is that all she said?"

He tilted his head back and looked down at her curiously. "What else would she have to say?"

Molly's lingering dread had escalated to near panic while she waited for Cole to show up. She ran a trembling hand over her face. "I don't know how to tell you this," she began falteringly.

"Why don't you start at the beginning?" he suggested gently.

"I'm pregnant." There. It was done. Swift and straight to the point. Mike and Barbara had been right, Molly thought. Whatever Cole's reaction, she felt better just getting the words out.

Whatever he'd been expecting, this was definitely not it. "Pregnant?" he asked in a mild enough voice. "With my child?"

"Who else's would it be?" Never, in her worst-case scenario, had Molly even considered that Cole might not believe the baby to be his.

"Who else's indeed," he murmured, feeling strangely shell-shocked. *A child. His child.* The thought was overwhelming. "I thought you said you were on the pill," he said, seeking something, anything, to say until his out-of-control pulse stopped ringing in his ears.

His careless words made Molly stiffen. "I was. And now that I've done my duty, I suppose I might as well go home."

Cole reacted to her brittle words like a sleepwalker. "What are you talking about?" he asked slowly, struggling to concentrate while his mind was still spinning. "You can't leave. We've too many plans to make."

"Plans?"

"Marriage, of course." Cole groaned inwardly at the unchivalrous way he'd found himself proposing. He'd been planning to ask Molly to marry him ever since that incredible morning when he'd realized that he loved her. But he'd hoped to do it with a great deal more class.

His gritty tone confirmed Molly's fears. "I'm not going to marry you, Cole."

His eyes narrowed. "The hell you aren't. Dammit, Molly, you're pregnant, and in my book that means marriage." *Terrific, Murdock,* he castigated himself. *Let's really turn on the charm.*

"Lots of single women have children these days," she argued.

"Lots of single women aren't having *my* child. Besides, in case you haven't noticed, sweetheart, I don't really give a damn about what other people do. Or think."

As much as Molly wanted to marry Cole, as often as she had fantasized about being his wife, dreamed of it, she had far too much pride to accept such a cold-blooded proposal. "In case *you* haven't noticed, times have changed, Cole. Women and children are no longer chattel, and pregnancy is no longer an excuse to enter into a loveless marriage."

"But I love you."

"And I love you."

He took off his black Stetson and ran his hand frustratedly through his thick dark hair. "Then what in the hell is the problem?"

It took every bit of Molly's resolve not to back down from Cole's blazing glare. "I've already suffered through one marriage based on all the wrong reasons. I'm not going to make the same mistake twice."

"Now you're comparing me to that jerk professor?" he asked incredulously.

"Of course not. I'm only pointing out that having to get married because I'm pregnant is a pretty shaky foundation for a marriage."

He couldn't believe he was hearing her correctly. "In the first place, since I don't see a father waiting in the wings with a shotgun, we're not *having* to get married. And in the second place, we love each other. So at the risk of sounding repetitive, where's the damned problem?"

"How about the little fact that you still don't entirely trust me?" she asked quietly.

"Of course I trust you."

"Really? Can you honestly tell me that you're not wondering if I lied to you about being on the pill?"

"I can unequivocally state that it never crossed my mind."

"Then why did you bring it up?"

"I said it without thinking. Dammit, Molly, you can't expect to drop a bombshell like this on a man and have him not react with a little surprise."

Molly remembered the shadow that had moved across his face. "It was more than surprise; you looked as though you'd just been sentenced to the electric chair."

"That had nothing to do with you." Frustration caused his next words to be rash. "I was thinking about Laura, dammit!"

The minute the words were out of his mouth, Cole knew they were the very worst thing he could have said. He watched a devastated Molly struggle to maintain her composure.

"I rest my case," she said quietly.

Before she could move, Cole had taken her stricken face in his hands. "Sweetheart, let me explain."

Cole knew the Fates were not on his side when Merle suddenly appeared in the doorway. "The plane's all gassed up, boss, and the sheriff's going to meet us at Horseshoe Bend."

Cole waved him away with an impatient hand. "Call the sheriff and tell him we're not coming. Something more important has come up."

"But, boss—"

"Tell him," Cole demanded gruffly.

"Sheriff?" Molly inquired after the Double Diamond's foreman had left. She had taken advantage of Merle's untimely interruption and moved to the other side of the room, away from Cole's beguiling touch.

Cole shrugged as he moved purposefully toward her. "We think the missing cattle are in Idaho. Seems a couple cowboys with a grudge against the Double Diamond decided to start their own business with our stock."

He cupped her shoulders with his hands. She was trembling and Cole wished he could say something that would get through to her. "I was going to check it out this afternoon. That's why I called, to let you know where I was going."

"Don't let me keep you." Molly knew she was handling this every bit as badly as Cole, but a strong sense of self-preservation kept her from admitting how badly his incautious words had hurt her.

As frustration soared to new heights, Cole was tempted to shake Molly. But he didn't. Because he loved her. And, he thought with that still overwhelming sense of wonder, she was going to have his baby.

"A few head of cattle aren't as important as this."

The despair in his dark eyes was moving, even though his first thought, on hearing the news, had been of his first wife. As much as Molly wanted to spend the rest of her life with this man, even this rambling ranch house wasn't big enough for the three of them: Cole, her and Laura.

"You've got rustlers to catch."

"They can wait. We need to talk."

"No, they can't. Not unless you want a good percentage of the stock slaughtered before you get there." When she tried to back away, his fingers tightened on her shoulders. "Go to Idaho, Cole."

Cole knew the effort it took for Molly to remain so calm, so composed, under such emotional pressure. Frustrated, he gave in to impulse and shook her once. Hard. "Would you quit being so damned hardheaded and hear me out."

"There's nothing left to say." The words sounded false, even to her own ears, but she was struggling to maintain some self-respect.

Muttering a short, desperate oath, Cole captured her mouth in a hard, hot, punishing kiss that showed no gentleness or mercy. His mouth ground against hers, his teeth nipped at her lips, his tongue plunged arrogantly past the barrier of her teeth, invading the dark recesses beyond. As his hands tangled in her hair, holding her in the devastating kiss, the passion that was driving him began seeping into her own bloodstream. With a soft moan that was part surrender, part desire, she quit fighting him. Her lips turned greedy as she began to return the heated kiss with a force that equaled Cole's.

"I could have you," he said, finally breaking the searing contact to bury his lips in the silken fragrance of her hair, "right now. In my bed, in my arms, crying out, begging me to take you."

His hand slowly trailed down her body, and he was rewarded as he felt her instinctive tremor. "No matter what you say, Molly, your reaction only proves what we've both known all along. That you're mine. And the baby will be mine, as well." Cole was determined to keep the past from repeating itself.

The masculine possessiveness in his tone should have irritated Molly. Instead, under the circumstances, it only deflated her hopes that anything could be accomplished here today. "People aren't possessions, Cole," she said quietly. "You can't buy them, and you can't keep them locked up in cages—physical or emotional—if they don't want to stay with you."

"Are you telling me that you've been lying all along? That you don't love me?" he demanded.

"Of course I love you," she insisted. "But I refuse to serve as a replacement for your ex-wife. Or worse yet, your mother."

His eyes widened, and his fingers tightened on her shoulders. "You're crazy."

She struggled against his hold. "I'd be crazy to marry you while you're still nursing whatever feelings you have for Laura. And your father's wife," Molly countered heatedly.

"I don't have any feelings for Laura, dammit! As for my mother, I never even knew her."

Molly shook her head. "Perhaps the part about your mother is getting a little Freudian," she admitted. "But you can't deny that Laura is still very much a part of your life. Not when you think of her every time you're with me." Fighting back bitter tears, she twisted out of his arms. "I'm going home now."

He let her get as far as the door. "Molly."

Stiffening her spine, as well as her resolve, she glanced back over his shoulder. "Yes?"

"I'll be gone two days, perhaps three. If you're not here when I get back, I'm coming after you."

Although Molly had a great many unanswered questions about her future with Cole, his words carried a warning that left no doubt about his intentions.

"Good luck in Idaho," she said, escaping from the room and the ranch before he put her resolve to the test.

13

BARBARA WAS WAITING FOR HER when she arrived home, and it took only one look at her stricken face for Molly to know that her day was going to continue its downhill slide.

"Don't tell me," she said as she got out of the car. "The hospital called."

"Your mother's been in an accident," Barbara confirmed grimly. "I called the ranch as soon as I heard, but Dallas said you'd already left." Her sympathetic expression turned openly speculative. "She also said that Cole was on his way to Idaho."

"He thinks he's found his missing cattle," Molly said flatly. "Did they tell you Loretta's condition?"

Barbara's blue eyes were awash with empathetic pain. "It's not good," she warned. "They're not expecting her to last the night."

Molly was suddenly so very, very tired. She dragged a trembling hand over her face. "I have to pack."

"It's all done." Barbara's usual competent manner was restored. "We had some trouble getting you on a flight out tonight—all the airlines were already double booked—but Mike and Gertie worked a little magic and issued you a ticket. All you have to do is show up and claim your seat."

"Mike broke into the airline's computer?"

"He was absolutely brilliant," Barbara said enthusiastically, smiling for the first time since Molly had pulled into the driveway. "By the way, you're flying first-class. Not that you'll be able to enjoy yourself under these circumstances. But at least you'll have a bit more privacy than you would back in economy."

The news of her pregnancy—had it only been a few hours ago?—along with her unsatisfactory encounter with Cole, topped by this not unexpected news of her mother, had left Molly too emotionally drained to fully express her gratitude. "Thank you," she whispered brokenly.

Barbara wrapped her arms around her and gave her a hard, reassuring hug. "Hey, what are friends for? Come on, you've got time for a cup of tea before Mike drives you to the airport."

UNLIKE THE CONTROLLED BEDLAM of the University of Oregon Medical Center in Portland, where Molly had recently spent so many anxious hours with Cole and Matt, there was an atmosphere of hushed calm about the Charleston sanatorium. The staff, dressed in street clothes, carried out their duties with remarkable efficiency, given the often unpredictable behavior of their patients.

Molly's first feelings upon seeing her mother were shock and dismay. It had been five months since she'd been to the clinic, and Loretta's condition had obviously deteriorated a great deal since then. Always a slender woman, she was now frighteningly thin, appearing almost anorexic. Her complexion had a faintly yellowish cast, which Dr. Wickes explained was caused by liver damage, and her blond hair was thin, with white roots. Her eyes were closed, her lashes resting on skin that reminded Molly of aged parchment.

As she sat down beside the bed, a soft moan escaped Molly's lips. "Damn you," she whispered, her lids stinging with angry, unshed tears, "damn you for doing this to yourself. To me." Her hand fluttered protectively over her still flat stomach. "To your grandchild."

Nothing. Molly had been warned that her mother had been drifting in and out of consciousness for the past six hours and therefore not to expect any positive response. As if she'd ever received any, Molly thought with a burst of anger and sorrow that was all too familiar. But compassion soon overrode those other confusing feelings, and Molly reached out, covering the bony hand on the crisp blue sheet with her own.

"I've met a man, Mama," she said in a halting but reasonably conversational tone, considering the circumstances. "I think you'd like him. No," she corrected with a slight smile, "I *know* you'd like him. He's a cowboy, like the ones you're always singing about. Actually, he's not exactly a cowboy, he's a rancher. In Oregon. His name is Cole Murdock." She took a deep breath. "And I love him, Mama, more than I ever thought possible."

Molly caught her breath when Loretta's hand seemed to move under hers, but when her mother's expression continued to be unresponsive, she decided she must have imagined it. "He's a good man. He's been hurt in love, but dear God, haven't we all?" Again there was that almost imperceptible movement, but still Loretta's eyes remained closed.

"I'm having his baby, Mama," Molly said in a soft rush of words. "And although I suppose I shouldn't be happy about it—not being married and all—I truly am. I don't exactly know how Cole feels," she admitted reluctantly. "We didn't really have time to talk about it, but he did ask me to marry him. Well, actually, it was more like he demanded that we get married, but you have to understand Cole to know that's just his way. He's used to making his own rules, but he really is a good man. And a loving one. And he'd make a wonderful father."

Molly breathed a sad, rippling little sigh. "I want to marry him, more than anything, but before I could tell him that, my damnable Hatfield pride got in the way and I insisted that I'd never give in to a shotgun wedding."

Her eyes misted with unshed tears at the memory of their last conversation. "What if he takes me at my word?" she asked. "What if he decides he doesn't want to marry me after all?"

She leaned forward, brushing some lank yellow strands of hair off her mother's forehead with gentle fingers. "It's scary, isn't it? I think I can understand how you felt, pregnant and all alone in a world that wasn't nearly so understanding about single women having babies. I used to hate you. I resented you for not wanting me. For not loving me. And these last few years, when you truly needed my help, I tried to be a good daughter, to take care of you like you never took care of me."

The tears that had been restrained too long began to flow. Molly brushed them away with the back of her hand. "But I don't hate you anymore," she whispered raggedly. "Partly because I love Cole so very, very much, and love and hate can't survive together." She drew in a deep breath as a feeling of peace settled over her. "But it's also because of the baby. Our baby, Cole's and mine." Her fingers curled more tightly around her mother's limp hand. "If it's a girl, I'm going to name her Sarah, Mama. After her grandmother."

This time Molly knew she wasn't imagining the pressure on her hand. Loretta's eyes fluttered open, and a single tear slid down her cheek like a silver ribbon.

"Sarah," she mouthed her agreement, managing something that could have been a smile.

Then Sarah Jane Pence closed her eyes for the last time. As Molly felt her mother's hand go limp in hers, she lowered her head to the sheet and wept unashamedly.

COLE MANEUVERED THE RENTAL CAR around the twisting switchbacks, wondering, not for the first time, if he was doing the right thing, descending on Molly without warning like this. But if there was one thing he didn't want to do, it was give her a chance to get away again. He'd already lost her once. He didn't think he'd ever get over the sinking feeling in his gut that he'd experienced after returning from Idaho only to find that Molly had run back home. When Barbara had informed him of the reason for her sudden departure, he'd experienced a wrenching guilt that the one time she had needed him—for his love, as well as his strength—he'd let her down.

Never again, he vowed as he crossed a rickety wooden bridge that had definitely seen better days; the wood creaked ominously as he inched the Ford across the covered span. From now on, at least until the baby was born, he wasn't going to let Molly out of his sight. Knowing Molly's flash-fire temper and frustrating intransigence all too well, Cole admitted that might be an impossible task. But he was going to marry her. And he was going to take care of her: watch that she ate a proper diet, make certain she took her vitamins, go to natural childbirth classes with her, all the things he'd been fantasizing about, looking forward to, during their recent separation.

For a man used to wide open spaces, Cole found the mountainous West Virginia countryside a revelation as he drove over ridge after ridge of rolling forested hills. Periodically he'd pass a small settlement where the weathered cabins and split-rail fences made him feel as if he'd stepped back in time. Cattle and ponies roamed at will along the roadside, and more than once he'd had to stop to let a white-tailed deer or a bandit-masked raccoon cross the road.

No, Cole thought, Molly's home wasn't anything like his own, but it definitely had its own overwhelming beauty; he found himself as taken with Molly's mountains as she had been with his wide sky and acres of rolling pastureland.

The asphalt ended. Following Billy Joe's verbal instructions, Cole kept following what was now a washboard-like dirt road, which he guessed had at least a hundred deep potholes, fifty ruts and ten washouts per mile. He'd been traveling for what seemed like hours— the sun was already dipping behind a mountain—when he heard a low ominous rumble on a distant ridge. Within minutes the area was covered by a canopy of fast-moving dark clouds that rolled through the mountain gaps. The thunder, once faint, now shook the tree-covered mountains. Rain streamed down the windshield, making visibility almost nil. But still he continued, determined to reach Molly before nightfall.

"Damn," he groaned as the car came to a shuddering halt. His front wheels had sunk into a ridiculously deep pothole, and as the tires settled into the mire, it became readily apparent that he'd have to make the rest of the journey on foot. Taking the flashlight out of the glove compartment, in case he was still on this isolated road come dark, Cole left the car and began slogging through the thick black mud.

MOLLY SAT OUTSIDE on the front porch of Billy Joe's rambling cabin and watched the storm as it clouded the velvet mountains in silver and black. "I'm glad the rain waited until after the funeral," she murmured.

"It would have been hard on folks getting there," Billy Joe agreed.

"I'm surprised so many came anyway. I never realized Mama had so many friends."

He reached out and took her hand. "They were your friends, Molly," he corrected quietly. "They've all missed you. Like Emma and I have."

A lump rose in her throat, and she took a sip of Emma's sassafras tea to clear it. "I've missed you, too."

He gave her a long, serious look. "But you're not staying, are you?"

"I can't." Her soft voice was close to a whisper. "I left a lot unsettled back in Oregon, Billy Joe. And if anyone should know that nothing good ever came from running away from your problems, it's me."

"Loretta was definite proof of that. Besides, you and that Cole Murdock fella should get your problems all straightened out before the baby comes. I love each and every one of my five kids, but let me tell you, Molly, if you're havin' problems, a new baby around the house will only make them seem worse."

She stared at him. "How on earth did you know about the baby?"

He looked a little sheepish. "Emma was the one who knew. She spotted it right off, soon as you walked in the door."

"How?"

He shrugged. "Could be some woman thing, I suppose. After all, she comes from a long line of midwives, so she should know something about the process, not to mention having five young uns of her own. Of course, you chucking your breakfast this morning was a bit of a clue," he said with a wink.

"I want this baby," she said firmly. Almost too firmly, Billy Joe thought. "But I have to admit my timing was less than ideal."

He laughed at that. "Molly, if any of us ever waited until the time was right, the world would've come to a screeching halt with Adam and Eve. Besides—" he squeezed her fingers reassuringly "—Cole's as thrilled as a hog in a mud waller over the prospect of being a father."

Molly stared at him. "Where did you get that idea? Have you been talking to Cole? Has he called? Did you call him? After I told you that I didn't want anyone to know where I was until I figured out what I was going to do?"

Billy Joe damned his fool tongue as he tried to think of a way to sidetrack Molly from knowing that he'd found himself siding with Cole Murdock ten minutes into last night's telephone conversation. Murdock was obviously head over heels in love with her, and if he'd ever heard a man so concerned about his bride-to-be and her baby, Billy Joe couldn't remember when.

He glanced down at his watch, then out into the driving sheets of rain, hoping that Cole would make it here in the next twenty minutes; otherwise, he'd have to go out searching for him. And from the looks of that storm, it wasn't something he was real eager to do. Not that he wouldn't, he told himself. For Molly. He'd loved Molly since the first day she'd arrived from the orphanage to help his mama out with the household chores, and if she'd seen fit to marry him, Billy Joe knew he never would have regretted it.

But *she* would have. In many ways Molly was a lot more like her mama than she'd admit. Both women wanted out of the mountains; the difference was that Molly's goals had been more realistic. And she'd been willing to work damned hard to achieve them. No, if she'd married him, she would have spent her life worrying about "what ifs."

Knowing all this, Billy Joe was content with the way things had worked out: he had his Emma, whom he'd never thought of as second choice, and five terrific kids, even if the house did seem to shake sometimes from the noise level generated by his three rambunctious sons and two equally spirited daughters.

For her part, Molly had gotten her coveted degree and was about to marry a man who Billy Joe had no doubt adored her. Just as he'd adore their child. So they'd both have families, and he could go on loving her as he always had.

"Billy Joe?" Molly's voice cut into his introspection. "You haven't answered my question. How do you know Cole's happy about the baby? That's sure not the impression I got the last time I saw him."

Knowing that he'd probably be damned for a liar, Billy Joe couldn't quite allow himself to meet Molly's probing gaze head-on. "Look, Molly, you say you're in love with him, and after marrying that professor jerk you'd never be stupid enough to make the same mistake twice, so this Cole fella must be a nice guy. Taking that into account, it only stands to reason that he'd want the baby you two made together, doesn't it?"

Molly continued to study him intently. "I suppose so," she said slowly. Her eyes started to mist again, and Molly realized that for a woman who never, ever cried, she was certainly doing a lot of it lately. "Oh, Billy Joe," she wailed, "I've really made a mess of things."

He took her in his arms, allowing her to vent her fears and sorrows as she wept inconsolably. When her sobs quieted, he continued to hold her, running his hand down her hair. "It's going to be okay," he assured her gruffly, feeling his own eyes growing suspiciously moist. "You've got to trust me, Molly. And know that I'd never do anything to hurt you."

Molly tilted her head back to study him curiously. She was about to speak when an all too familiar voice made her heart leap into her throat.

"Thank God. I thought I'd never find you."

"Cole!" She jumped up and spun around, staring at him standing only a few feet away. His black hair was plastered to his head, his clothes were soaked, and water was streaming down his face in rivulets. Dark shadows beneath his eyes showed that he hadn't been getting any more sleep than she, and the rough planes of his face appeared tight and drawn. She started to run to him, then stopped, suddenly aware that he'd caught her in another man's arms. So much for trust.

"This is Billy Joe," she managed to get out through lips that had gone as dry as dust. "He's—"

"I know who he is," Cole answered easily, dragging his gaze from Molly to the silent man standing behind her. He held out his hand. "It's good to meet you, Billy Joe."

"Same here," Molly's longtime friend answered as he accepted Cole's outstretched hand. "I think you two could do with some privacy. I'll try to keep the kids in the house."

"Thank you." Cole's gaze had drifted back to Molly's face. "Oh, did you check on that little detail I asked about?"

"Sure did," Billy Joe said. "How's tomorrow morning, ten o'clock, sound?"

"Perfect. I'll call the others in a few minutes and fill them in." Cole smiled broadly, satisfaction evident in his expression. "Thank you," he repeated gravely. "For everything."

Billy Joe's face split in a broad grin. "My pleasure," he said before leaving them alone.

"What was that all about?" Molly asked.

Cole didn't immediately answer her question. "I'll tell you in a minute," he said, drawing her into his arms. "First things first."

He lowered his head, and for a long, luxurious time there was only pleasure—a bright, gleaming, golden pleasure—as if the sun had suddenly come out from behind the rain clouds. Molly clung to Cole, reveling in the taste of his lips, the feel of his strong, familiar body pressing into hers.

"God, I've missed you," he said finally.

"Not as much as I've missed you."

"Want to bet?" Unable to resist, Cole drew her mouth back to his. When he lifted his head, his dark eyes were grave. "I'm sorry about your mother."

Pain showed in her eyes, but a newfound peace was there, as well. "We didn't have that much time together, but I think we managed to salvage something in the end."

His fingers were infinitely tender as they brushed away some blond hair that had fallen into her eyes. "I'm glad. There's something I have to explain. About Laura."

Molly put her hand on his chest. "You don't have to explain anything, Cole. I overreacted."

"Perhaps we both did," Cole murmured, covering her slender hand with his. "But it's important that you understand." With as few words as necessary, Cole explained about Laura's abortion and the pain he'd suffered because of it.

"When you told me that you were pregnant," he said quietly, his serious black eyes holding hers, "all I could think was that it had to be a miracle. I never believed that I'd ever have a second chance for a family."

"Oh, Cole," Molly said on a soft sigh, "I do so love you."

"And I love you. So are you going to marry me?"

A ghost of a smile curved the corners of her mouth. "That all depends," she said slowly, consideringly. "Are you asking?"

"I'm asking," he assured her huskily, nipping at her lower lip.

"Well, in that case, I suppose I'll accept. When?"

Cole ran his hand slowly down her side, pleased beyond reason by her responsive tremor. "I was thinking around ten o'clock tomorrow morning might be nice."

Pleasure shone in Molly's green eyes. "You and Billy Joe were in on this together, weren't you?"

"Guilty. But we weren't exactly alone."

"Oh?"

When he lifted her hand and kissed her fingers, one at a time, a shimmering warmth spread through her. "Barbara and Mike are spending the night in a hotel in Charleston. What would you say to a double wedding?"

Laughing, Molly flung her arms around his neck. "I'd say yes," she said against his lips. "Yes, yes, yes."

THE HOSPITAL STAFF CHEERED in unison as they watched the bright red apple slowly drop in Times Square on the television in the nurses' lounge. With pieces of colorful confetti scattered in her hair and the strains of "Auld

Lang Syne" ringing in her ears, Barbara Baker sent the following telegram to Billy Joe Pence:

Pop the Champagne. Sarah Kristine Murdock and William Garrett Murdock arrived shortly after midnight. Mother and babies in terrific shape. Father expected to recover.

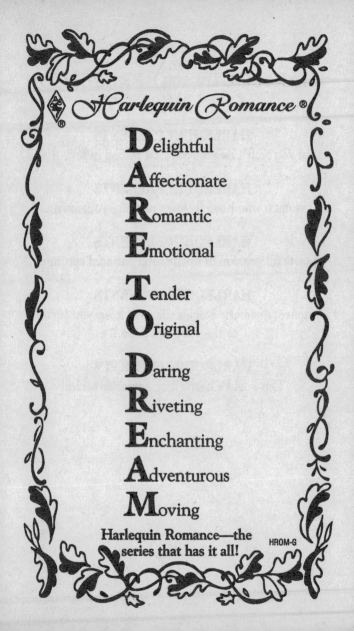

Harlequin Romance ®

Delightful

Affectionate

Romantic

Emotional

Tender

Original

Daring

Riveting

Enchanting

Adventurous

Moving

Harlequin Romance—the
series that has it all!

HROM-G

HARLEQUIN PRESENTS

HARLEQUIN PRESENTS
men you won't be able to resist falling in love with...

HARLEQUIN PRESENTS
women who have feelings just like your own...

HARLEQUIN PRESENTS
powerful passion in exotic international settings...

HARLEQUIN PRESENTS
intense, dramatic stories that will keep you turning
to the very last page...

HARLEQUIN PRESENTS
The world's bestselling romance series!

LOOK FOR OUR FOUR FABULOUS MEN!

Each month some of today's bestselling authors bring four new fabulous men to Harlequin American Romance. Whether they're rebel ranchers, millionaire power brokers or sexy single dads, they're all gallant princes—and they're all ready to sweep you into lighthearted fantasies and contemporary fairy tales where anything is possible and where all your dreams come true!

You don't even have to make a wish...Harlequin American Romance will grant your every desire!

Look for Harlequin American Romance wherever Harlequin books are sold!

SILHOUETTE® Desire®

Do you want...

Dangerously handsome heroes

Evocative, everlasting love stories

Sizzling and tantalizing sensuality

Incredibly sexy miniseries like **MAN OF THE MONTH**

Red-hot romance

Enticing entertainment that can't be beat!

You'll find all of this, and much *more* each and every month in **SILHOUETTE DESIRE**. Don't miss these unforgettable love stories by some of romance's hottest authors. Silhouette Desire—where your fantasies will always come true....

If you've got the time...
We've got the
INTIMATE MOMENTS

Passion. Suspense. Desire. Drama. Enter a world that's larger than life, where men and women overcome life's greatest odds for the ultimate prize: love. Nonstop excitement is closer than you think...in Silhouette Intimate Moments!